Sophisticated Swingers

Adult Erotic Fiction

Book One - Couples

Michelle Browne

Sophisticated Swingers

Book One - Couples

Adult Erotic Fiction by Michelle Browne

Copyright © 2014 by Michelle Browne

Visit Michelle's Blog: www.sophisticatedswingers.org

Michelle Browne/Shipyard Press

www.shipyardpress.com

ISBN 978-0-9910678-1-7

Publisher's Note: This is a work of fiction. Names, characters, places, and incidents are a product of the author's imagination. Locales and public names are sometimes used for atmospheric purposes. Any resemblance to actual people, living or dead, or to businesses, companies, events, institutions, or locales is completely coincidental.

Table of Contents

1

MICHELLE

"WHAT'S WRONG DANNY?" I had to shout in his ear to make him hear me over the boat's engine and it didn't sound right.

"Damned if I know," he shouted back, fiddling with the throttle to try to smooth the engine out.

"I think you've picked up some sea grass in the prop," Jeff shouted over the din from his seat near the stern.

"Could be—hang on, I'm going to try for that little strip of sand over there, we can stop and have a look." he shouted back while jiggling the throttle to keep the engine running and put us on that sliver of beach. We bumped up on to the sand just as the engine gave it's last gasp—*I'm done,* it was saying.

Danny leaned over the stern of his boat to inspect the prop problem. His shoulder-length, straight, black hair fell over his face. I love when his hair gets in the way of, well . . . whatever it is he's doing. He tossed it back out of his eyes with a flick of his head.

"Michelle, this may take a while," he grumbled, after seeing the dripping mess trapped in the propeller. I could tell he was really bummed. We had planned today's excursion on the water to show off his new boat and get our friends Heather and Jeff together for a late lunch at the Tiki Hut, a favorite beachside bar. Amy, our third musketeer was also invited to bring along her new heartthrob, Kevin. Giving us all a chance to meet him.

"Why don't you girls explore the beach while we untangle this stuff and check for damage, it's a hell-of-a-mess back here." As he peered over the stern his tight butt capping those lean muscular thighs in sailing shorts didn't hurt my eyes either!

"OK, lover boy," I drawled slowly, but on purpose. My Southern accent always turned Danny on and he flashed me a smile in spite of his obvious irritation. Kevin the new guy, and Jeff, hopped out of the boat, splashing each other for a moment before wading around to the stern to help Danny. Jeff had a boat and was a little older and more experienced on the water than Danny so he took the initiative and after a good look at the mess around the outdrive unit and he pronounced it, "Another-first-class, cluster-fuck." Hearing that, Heather, my friend since high school frowned sadly, looking away. He was obviously continuing some sort of tiff they had going on since before they came aboard. I knew that look and were those dark circles or just eye shadow under her eyes?

Amy on the other hand was all smiles, glowing as her new beau Kevin came over to the side and helped us girls out of the boat and into the shallow water. He was nice, I liked him. I think she does also, it's been nearly two years since she and Jim divorced and she needs someone new in her life, someone besides her ex, Jim who lives just a few blocks away and shares custody raising their two kids. Even though she got the house free and clear in the divorce settlement, It's got to be hard making ends meet and raising kids on just her newspaper advertising commissions and a little child support.

I led the way splashing through the shallows to the beach, which could not have been silkier, a pure crystalline white. The recent storms must have buffed it clean of everything but the heavier quartz granules, every one of which glistened in the sun. There was nothing to do here on this tiny beach except grab some rays and watch the guys work on the boat so I decided to get comfy; there was no one around except our own party of fun-in-the-sun seekers. I went back onboard for some beach gear. Kevin saw me and once again came over to help me on and off the boat. He's good, I like him. Our brightly colored beach towels hit the sand and Heather and I followed. Amy, attracted by just watching Kevin, wandered back into the water to watch the boys work on clearing the boat's propeller of grass. When Amy was out of earshot I asked Heather, "What's with you two, you and Jeff that is, care to tell me about it?"

"No it's nothing," she said.

"It must be something," I said, "or your eyes wouldn't look like spacey black holes. I've known you long enough to know when you're upset Heath, come-on spill!" She looked at me with pleading eyes, I could tell she wanted to tell me but also wanted it to, *"just go away!"*

She changed the subject to, "Let's get some rays, I don't want to waste this sunshine dwelling on things in the past. With that she untied the bikini string behind her back and somewhat defiantly folded her top and put it at the foot of her towel.

Just then Amy came bouncing back up the beach, hand in hand with Kevin, both of them happily smiling. *"You can tell when people are in love,"* I thought, *"there is really no hiding it."*

Amy repositioned her towel, leaving room for Kevin on the outside and stretched out her petite body for maximum effect. No one would ever guess she had given birth to two children, no belly fat, no stretch marks, nothing!

"They don't need me," Kevin said nodding toward the boat, "Dan and Jeff are the boating experts, I only putz around on Jet Ski's, nothing too complicated there. They'll have that grass cleared up any day now," he leered at Heather as he flopped down on the sand next to Amy. "Besides I want to hear some more about this club you girls found, what's it called . . . The Palms?"

"What! What club," I wanted to know; I was all ears now as earlier on the boat I had overheard Amy and Heather talking about "the club" whatever it was.

But Kevin was not finished, "In due time, Michelle, in due time, but first I believe there is a big mystery going on here. Somewhere there may be a place called 'The Palms' and that's supposed to be a secret, and now Heather is exposing her ta-ta's to this red blooded American boy and he's not supposed to look while his girlfriend lying next to her is all covered up and hiding all sorts of delights behind a thin veil of no touchee-no feelee, and next to her is another beautiful southern belle also hiding her ta-ta's from the sun which I can hear crying through that thin fabric, *Let us out! Let us out!* They are just pleading to be free. Tell me there is no mystery going on here?"

"Should we tell her?" Amy tittered, her sky blue eyes shining with mischief.

Heather couldn't resist coming out of her funk and with an impish grin, untied the strings of her bikini top while looking at me with those dark eyes.

"What!" I wasn't playing this game.

Just then Danny waded through the water to the other side of the boat to get something out of his toolbox, catching this last comment and looking at Amy and Heather now topless said,

"Well?"

His "thing" for Heather was never more apparent.

I had no choice, my top followed.

"Ok, Ok," Kevin announced, "I'm getting out of here before this stripping spreads to boxers," he said hiking up his shorts and wading back in the water to help the boys.

Clothing crisis averted, Amy, Heather and I lay back to soak in some major rays since it looked like it would take the guys a while longer to clear the prop. I loved that both of my BFFs were blondes while I was the only brunette, the shade so deep brown most people thought my hair was black. I stretched out slowly but Amy and Heather started giggling about something, piquing my curiosity . . . Finally I lifted my head and shielding my eyes against the hot sun I had to ask, "Ok What is it now, what's going on with you two, is it about this 'club' you call it?"

"Should we tell her?" Amy tittered, her sky blue eyes shining with mischief.

"I don't know, do you think Michelle can handle it?" Heather ventured.

"Handle what? Come on you two, what are you hiding?" I pressed. I sat up. "Ok, Ok," Amy said, sitting cross-legged now, "scoot closer and we'll tell you where we're supposed to go next Saturday."

"Saturday night too, maybe," Heather chimed in, giggling anew.

"Well, what is it already . . . go where?" I demanded. "Are you going to keep me in the dark forever?"

Amy leaned closer. "We're going to a swing club," she confessed.

"A what?"

"A swinger's club, Michelle. It's called Tropical Palms," Heather announced. "And it's right here in town too. Who knew?"

"A swinger's club," I repeated. "How on earth did you find that here of all places? But more importantly, what are you planning to do there?"

They both tried to talk at once but Heather quickly won out; she'd been a big gabber since our sorority days together. "We have this friend, I don't think you know her, a hairdresser at the salon where I go sometimes, you know, to get something special." She raked a hand through her mane of thick blond hair. "Anyway, her name is Julie and last time I saw her, she asked if I was Amy's best friend.

"'I see you two together sometimes walking past our window,' she said. 'You're a beautiful, sexy pair and I was wondering if you'd like to meet some other sexy people in a comfortable setting and sort of play around, you know, safely?'"

Amy uncrossed her long legs slowly, and I watched Kevin in the water watching her and he gave her one of his smoldering looks. The muscles across his bare chest flexed. Was he showing off or was that just his buff construction body getting excited?

Heather had not stopped talking. "Well, I was so surprised I couldn't answer right away. I had to think about what she'd said for a second. Then I asked, "What other people, and just what do you mean, play around safely?"

"Well, Julie went on about how she and her significant other had been going to a private party in someone's home for a couple of years now. Instead of playing bridge or card games they flirt, they dance, swim and have sex with anyone who's there, no questions asked. There's no jealousy, and no consequences. It's a completely adult party, no pressure, no forcing anything on anyone, just free and easy sex with whomever you please, married or not. They enjoy it so much, she said, that they feel like missionaries."

Amy snickered. She was an Army brat who had lived all over the world and clearly thought this allusion to swingers as missionaries was comical.

"That's what she said," Heather continued. "They want to let the world know that there's an outlet for all the sexual tension, repression and cheating that's going on in the world. A place where sex is just sex, and nobody is hung up about doing it with whomever they please."

"Wow . . . that sounds like, well, Utopia," I said.

Heather's face lit up. "It kinda is." She went on about how Julie had said that she and her lover had become really tight, good friends with a lot of the members and would like to include us if we were interested. "She said she knew we would like the other people, that they were just like us . . . and that Amy and I would like it a lot. Right, Ames?"

"Absolutely!" Amy saluted.

Heather laughed. "She said if we were interested we should give her our phone number and that we would be contacted by the house hostess and invited to a short seminar on the weekend where we'd learn what it was all about. After I talked it over with Amy, we thought it wouldn't hurt to go and just check it out."

Amy nodded as Heather chattered on.

"We thought, its just talk and might be fun, right? So I gave Julie my cell number. I didn't want anyone in my family answering my house phone and getting details about a 'swing club', can you imagine? Jeff would've killed me."

We all took a moment to watch Jeff, the most serious-minded of the group, try to take a subservient role and assist Danny. Jeff was a high-powered computer exec and though he knew how to have a good time during his off hours, his current scowl let us know that this was not his favorite moment of the day.

Heather stifled a laugh. "Well, a few days later I got the call from a very nice lady named Angelea. Let me tell you she didn't hesitate to start spilling it about 'The Palms.' She invited us to come to their house around noon the following Saturday. There'd be a few others there, both members and guests like ourselves. A free brunch was planned and afterward, if we wanted to stay, we could hear all about the club and how it operated. She stressed that there would be no real names, no nudity, no stripping and no sexual play at the 'orientation'. And there was no selling of any kind, nothing to buy! It was just a chance to become acquainted with each other and answer questions in a no-stress atmosphere."

Amy had not stopped nodding encouragingly while Heather continued. "I called Amy right away; she'd just gotten the same call. We decided we'd let the boys decide if we should go, but I definitely wanted to check it out. It sounded like fun, and since we're all adults, a little spice can't hurt, right? When I started telling Jeff about the call he said he'd heard there was a swingers group in our town but didn't know anything more about it. You know, Jeff knows a little bit about everything going on around here. So, long story short, we decided to go if Amy and Kevin would go with us. That night Amy called back and said they were in."

"So, that's what we're doing next Saturday," Amy whispered. "Are you jealous or what?"

"Well, I . . . don't know . . ." I hesitated. "Maybe sex parties are way out of this old married woman's league."

"Oh Michelle, don't be so uptight!" Heather chided. "Out of all of us you're always the one up for a party! Maybe we all can go one time at least . . . just to check it out."

She was right of course. "Party" could have been my middle name, but this was something I'd never done. "I mean, I don't know," I finally said. "The thought of a bunch of bouncy bimbos and horny guys with who knows what kind of diseases pawing me and Danny might not be my idea of fun."

"Oh come on, Michelle, it's not like that," Amy said. "Nearly everyone we know is creeping up on middle age with kids at home or away in school, and all of us have started losing that old spark in the bedroom, although with Kevin . . ." her voice trailed off, then she giggled!

Now it was Heather's turn to nod in agreement. "If we don't do something to meet new people and try new things we'll all just grow old and gray and wonder one day what happened to all this . . ." She spread her arms to encompass the scene. We all gazed at the men with their shirts off, still soaking wet from their impromptu water fight.

Amy sighed. "If you want, Heather and I will take notes and let you know how it goes."

Just then Danny called out, "OK, we got it, we're good to go. All aboard, folks!" We jumped up, slipped back into our tops and shook the sand from our towels, and then were back on the water, cruising the bay again toward the Tiki Hut directly now. The motor drowned out the possibility of any more conversation at that moment. In addition to the naked torsos of our men and the gorgeous day around us I couldn't shake the new and different sexy images that started to fill my mind's eye as I looked over at the rosy glow on both Amy and Heather's cheeks. As we sped across the channel, I knew I was not alone.

THE NEXT SATURDAY, Amy called early,

"Heath?"

"Yeah?"

"I'm terrified . . . I'm not sure I want to do this and besides, I have no idea what to wear to this . . . orientation?"

I had no idea either and could only offer, "It sounded like sexy outfits are not particularly called for, at least for this brunch . . . so what do you think, Bermuda's with a blouse?"

"I think so, pants for sure . . . in case we have to run."

"Oh come on, you think?"

"No silly, but Bermuda's might be more comfortable, I'm going with that." Of course it was easy for the boys, their usual baggy cargo shorts and knit shirts.

Kevin and Amy drove over a little early and we killed time out on the patio with an IPA just for courage, giving us a chance to learn a little more about Kevin. He and Amy were practically joined at the hip now and they couldn't keep their hands off each other. I noticed Jeff smiling,

"Ain't young love grand!" he said giving me a hug when we got up to go.

Out in the driveway Kevin's Mercedes CLK was blocking our garage.

"Ride with us, I'll drive, we don't need two cars."

We all piled in and Kevin drove to the address the hostess had given. Surprisingly, it was only about a mile from our house, just another large, slightly Spanish style house on a street full of nice houses, much like the rest of South Florida. One man, out mowing his lawn, tossed us a wave as we went by (a knowing wave when I thought about his smile later.) This section of town was a little older and houses were larger than those on our street, being set back further with larger front yards. Kevin spotted the place first, and with three cars already in the circular drive, it kinda made us wonder how many people were coming. Some other houses on the street were graced with circular driveways like this one and all sported two or three car garages and probably a boat canal in back. It definitely was a more expensive part of town than where we lived. We were a little self-conscious piling out of Kevin's SUV and walking up to the green front door and yes, the gorgeous carved door was stained dark green. But before we could ring the bell it opened presenting a smiling man with a brush of grey hair at the temples. His creamy white Cuban Guayabera over tropical slacks and sandals just oozed class.

"Hi, I'm Robert," he said smiling, then turning slightly, "And this is my wife Angelea," letting a trim well-tanned woman into the entryway.

"Hello people," she smiled, "I'm the one who called you. Won't you please come in?"

She then pointed to a side hall table with nametags lined up, and said, "If you will put on your name tag we won't have to go through awkward introductions all day." There were four tags there with our first names only, simple enough. When we were all properly tagged, Robert introduced themselves again, and using our first names, "Amy and Kevin, Heather and Jeff welcome to our home, I'm Robert and this is my wife Angelea. We are both very happy you came and glad to have you here."

So smooth, I thought, but Amy tittered, and Jeff blushed again. Kevin remained silent, though I saw him glancing again at the backside of the green door, which had a clear rubbed oil finish. Kevin whispered to Amy,

"That door is swietenia mahogany, the rarest of rare tropical woods, cool!" Robert led us into their large step-down living room decorated in a refined Spanish style, elegant as the outside. From the ceilings massive wooden roof beams, to the tile floors covered with plush wool throw rugs, the room a handmade feel, as if the builder lovingly fashioned this house just for himself. *"Not bad,"* Kevin said under his breath. Jeff grabbed my hand again. Amy oohed. The furniture was clustered in small conversation groups, low leather sofas, lots of pillows with leather hassocks and smallish square low stools for sitting. A neutral shade of gray covered the walls allowing the accessories, lamps and some oil paintings, to proclaim their own beauty. It was obviously professionally decorated with a subtlety that spoke of an artistic hand. One wall, entirely made of glass, looked out to a pool and patio and beyond that, a high privacy wall with lots of landscaping. It was a comfortable room, tasteful, and welcoming. We quickly relaxed.

There were three other couples sitting quietly, we supposed waiting for us before things could start. As Robert brought us into the room, he said, "Ok, we're all here now. If you would please introduce yourselves and make yourselves comfortable, we'll get started in a minute. Angelea and I are so happy you all are here."

I fell in love with Jeff all over again as he finally released my hand from his and began to introduce himself and me to all the other couples. He was Mr. Professional, and although he blushed the whole time, he was smooth as silk introducing us to these other folks. Kevin didn't move until Amy followed in Jeff's footsteps and graciously reached both hands toward the others. She was Ms. World Traveler at ease anywhere. We met Scott and Amanda, Adam and Wendy and another couple, Burt and Betty I think. Then we found seats on a sofa or one of the leather stools, sat and waited. Robert stood off to one side looking like a proud papa. He was obviously pleased with our little group. When introductions were finished and everybody was seated, Robert said, "Can I offer anyone something to drink, coffee, water or soft drink?" No takers. Angelea slid quietly onto the sofa next to me. *Mmmm, what was that perfume?* She smelled heavenly.

"Ok, well, let's get started then, I know you're interested or you wouldn't be here. So let me give you a brief history and a little background of swinging; sexual sharing or polyamory as it is sometimes called, then we'll have a bit to eat and continue on if you like. This is a fun journey I'm sure you will agree, talking about sex or sexual sharing is something we've all dreamed some fantasy about at one time or another so today Angelea and I will try to answer your questions as to why and how it works," he continued . . . today will be a fun trip that may very well change the rest of your life," he grinned, just exuding optimism.

"Apparently, and no one knows exactly because no one was writing these things down, but sometime in the early 1940's on a military base out West, some junior officers living on base with their young wives, cut off from their hometowns, friends and families, bored, and with no money and nowhere to spend it if they'd had any, began having weekend parties. After an evening of drinking, dancing, and flirting the sexual energy would be over the top. Someone probably grabbed all the car keys off a hall table and throwing them in a bowl on a coffee table declared a new game, "wife-swap." The wives present would pick a set of keys from the bowl and then go for an hour or two, or even overnight with the owner of the keys. That method of mixing things up worked pretty well until someone balked or was unwilling to go with a particular owner of the keys."

"Maybe she just didn't like his car," Angelea laughed.

With a sideways smile at her (like I've heard that before) he continued, "A better way needed to be found. Many attempts to refine the process have been tried by other groups of friends. Today it has evolved into two basic forms of swinging, a term that came into use in the early 1960's, out of the hippie movement when "free love" was making the rounds. Eventually the term, "Lifestyle" has come to represent swinging today.

One of the other new couples—younger of the two pairs—was a shaved headed guy in a skin tight T-shirt that kept staring at Michelle. He was with a wisp of a thing whose waist length straight black hair falling against her alabaster white skin made her quite striking. She kept shifting position as Robert spoke, a fidgeter.

"One group favors commercial clubs. "Plato's Retreat," being one of the early ones in New York City and there were others.

"I've heard of that!" It was Pocahontas of the long black hair. Robert smiled patiently. Her beau leaned back against the pillows and opened his legs. *"My, My,"* I thought, *"look who brought a nice big gift to the party."*

"Of course," Robert said. "Well, today there are resorts and sometimes cruise ships where couples are free and encouraged to have sex with anyone else at the club, or on board the ship. The rules for this are simple, "Let the buyer beware!" You probably wouldn't know these other people beforehand; they could be from anywhere, from across the country or wherever? You don't know their lifestyle either; for instance, are they into bad behavior, rough sex, drugs or worse? You have no idea of their sexual history, and more importantly you may never see them again, even if you wanted to. It's scary when you think about it but don't let me frighten you, there is an alternative and it's groups like us.

We are a private group of people of like mind and background who share our partners with others in a closed, safe environment. We are local, we live here, we are not into risky behavior, we are healthy, loving, and protective and can be trusted. These folks around you today, and others you may meet in the future will possibly become your very best of friends, friends you will share everything with, or they may not . . . but you will have a connection with them that usually doesn't usually exist among "just friends" and surely not on board a ship or at a resort in the tropics."

"I couldn't help but notice Scott (or was it Scotty?) across from us salivating on Amy's long legs stretching out from her Bermuda's. I shouldn't be jealous of her, she is my friend, but I could kill for legs like that."

"Let's take a breath, any questions so far?" Robert asked.

Mr. Big Bulge finally sat up with a grunt and brought his legs together, looking only at Pocahontas. She only shrugged. The rest of us looked at each other or at the wool floor rugs with nervous smiles.

Still touching, sitting next to me, Angelea chimed in, "This is a wonderful journey of discovery for both partners, I think you will see what I mean later on but first, is anybody hungry? Let's have a snack before we get into the fun stuff, words and music, I mean, no touching today, and don't even think about breaking the rules!" Laughing an infectious laugh, Angelea rose and led the way to the dining room where a light buffet graced the table.

Food broke the ice as we clustered around the table filling our plates with delicious, tasty morsels and using the opportunity, sneaking a peek at the other couples around the table.

"Just sit anywhere," Angelea said, "Maybe this is a good chance to visit with and meet your new friends." And with that she and Robert disappeared into the kitchen leaving us alone to chat and enjoy our lunch.

As Jeff filled his plate with fresh sliced turkey, some fruit and cheese, he said, "well, I don't know about the rest of you, but so far this is terrific," indicating the delectable buffet and the attractive people around it. There was no question that everyone there, in their own way, was quite appealing. Even that older couple, neither of who had not yet said a word.

"Thanks for breaking the ice, Jeff. Amanda and I are looking forward to meeting you and your wife . . . Amy, is that right?"

That was Scott, the one who had ogled Amy's legs earlier. He was an All-American type, with thick shoulders that made me wonder what it'd be like to cry on—or better yet, straddle them. Whoa, I couldn't believe I was thinking these thoughts!

Amy smiled. "Hi Scott, you have a good memory . . . or good eyesight. Let's go find a place to sit." After filling a plate, Scott and Amy headed back to the living room, trailed by Kevin and Amanda.

I stayed at the buffet table, working up the nerve to say hello to Mr. Big Bulge and Pocahontas. She was interesting, him not so much. The older couple had started to chat Jeff up. I noticed him blushing again; though definitely older than us, the wife (her diamond was big enough to notice across the room) looked like Bette Midler in her prime. We are talking knockers to knock your socks off!

Amy found a small club table with four bamboo chairs. Never one to hold back, she said, "It's nice to meet someone new in town. We seem to see the same faces month after month." She giggled, "Not that we've been here before."

Amanda smiled. "I know what you mean. We're new in town so everyone and . . . all this is new to us. Scott just got transferred here by his company," she giggled!

"Oh yeah? Who's that?" Kevin asked.

"Phosphate, Inc.," Scott said, "Know them?"

"Not really, they have a mining operation out east of town don't they?"

"Yeah, that and a whole bunch of other related things."

"I'm with a builder, maybe we can do something for you one day?"

"That'd be good, get out and make contacts my boss said, although I'm not sure he meant like this," Scott said, waving his hand around, grinning.

"Well, already you've met some new people, us and those other folks that were here when we came in," Amy said impishly, "I dare you to go back and tell your boss where your spent your Saturday meeting people."

Laughing, "No, I think not, but I appreciate the suggestion. We're brand new to this—swinging or lifestyle; I don't quite know what to call it. I think Amanda and I will just keep this our little secret, thank you!"

"I think we all have some learning to do today and it's so exciting that I'm all tingly," Amy said as she poked Kevin in the ribs who, grinning, poked her back.

The two other couples joined Heather and Jeff as they spread themselves over a sofa, hassock and a stool. They were soon busy working on the food and checking out their lunch mates. Conversation naturally started with where are you from, have you lived here long, how did you find out about the Palms, have you done this before, and most importantly, what do you think?

One couple was a little older and quiet. They didn't seem at all shy or embarrassed and weren't grinning as much, just concentrating on their lunch and listening. Finally at a lull in the conversation, he spoke up,

"It's fun meeting new people . . . people new to swinging. My wife Wendy and I are not new, we've been in another group locally that just wasn't working for us," Adam said. "We've heard about the Palms and Wendy met Angelea once at another party so we finally decided to call her and ask if we could join the group, and here we are."

"So . . . in the other group you just swapped wives, how does that happen?" Kevin asked.

"Well obviously this is a much more structured group than the other one," Adam went on, "Angelea said we must attend an orientation seminar before being ask to join. In the other group, you just came to parties and sorted it out yourself."

"Adam," Wendy said, "Kevin asked about how our last group worked . . . exchanging partners and such. Can you answer him or do you want me to?"

"I'm sorry Kevin, I wasn't paying attention. No, it's not really swapping wives, it's called 'partying' as in, 'would you like to party with me,' except some folks in that group just wanted to fuck, to put it plainly. That was turning us off with some people. We wanted a little more romance in our encounters, Wendy in particular." He went on, "It's a little like dating, only your dates are short and more to the point, so to speak," he said, chuckling.

Wendy spoke up, "The Lifestyle is a wonderful way to keep the excitement alive, even long after you have grown accustomed to your partner or husband. We're not newbies at sex, both of us were married before and obviously before that we probably were in relationships that were all about sex, well maybe not all, but when you are young, sex is important, you agree?" she asked, getting grins.

"The other thing," Wendy went on, "Is the people we now mostly enjoy, are our swinging friends. We can talk about anything with them, there are no suspicions, everything is open, I mean, when you are naked and having sex with someone, you're usually not hiding anything, right?"

"But don't you get jealous sometimes?" Amy asked, admiring Wendy's openness and inner radiance when she was talking about swinging. It certainly seemed to agree with Adam also, he was beaming from ear to ear and flooding love on his wife with his eyes.

"Only when he's having more fun than me!" Wendy giggled.

Amy and Heather exchanged glances across the room, both girls were settling in to this new situation and the smiles on their faces told the world it was more than ok with them. Heather, sitting next to Jeff, was intently listening to the conversation between a very pretty Bette Midler type lady sitting next to him and a man on the other side. The other lady in that group, the one with the long straight black hair was quiet, her husband doing all the talking and so loud it sounded like boasting. Lunch continued on and by the time Robert and Angelea came back in the room, most were finished eating.

"Everybody have enough to eat?" Robert asked as he and Angelea went around picking up plates and glasses. Soon the room was cleared and doors to the kitchen hid all the mess. "Two bathrooms are down the hall this way," pointing, "And there is one out near the front door. We'll start again in about five minutes if that is ok with everyone." With that he walked to the sliding glass doors opening to the pool and went outside for a smoke. All the girls went down the hall to use a bathroom and gossip while nervousness and too much ice tea at lunch made the boys seek out the front hall half-bath.

WHEN THE SLIDING DOORS OPENED AGAIN, Robert came in and apologized, "I'm trying to quit," he explained, "Down to just one cigarette a day, noontime is my fix time, sorry." Then, "Is everybody ready to start again?" It was both a question and a statement. You could tell Robert was used to running meetings, he wasted no time getting to the point.

He began, "Swinging is not just fucking other women." His use of the f-word was meant to be shocking, and it was. He went on, "We bring our wives and significant others into this in a loving-sharing way in a protected, loving group like ours. Both partners can have that variety that anticipation, that "different" experience and be completely open in a non-jealous way. Lack of jealously is one of the keystones of this lifestyle. Even though everyone carries a little bit of jealously in their lives. We're jealous of the demands of time, of kids, and of a mother-in-law who still wants her daughter underfoot. We're jealous of the neighbor who seems to have a prettier or younger wife, or a newer car, or of a co-worker who seems to get away with stuff that he or she shouldn't and the big one, jealously when we think our mate might be flirting with someone else, even if it's just for fun. But the worst kind of jealousy is that of trying or wanting to control our partners' feelings. Sometimes we want our partner to like something or like somebody, just because we do. Or, what is worse . . . to not like something or someone just because we have made up our minds and expect our partner to feel the same. This is particularly true in personal relationships. We may or may not feel the same way about someone our partner enjoys being with, even if only socially, but one thing we learn to do in swinging is to . . . let go, to let it be . . . .

"Allowing our partner complete freedom in choosing who to have a relationship with, if only for a few minutes here in the confines of our group, is intensely liberating to ourselves. Each of us is no longer responsible for our partner's choices—and when we cannot be judgmental or controlling about whom they (or we) choose to enjoy and perhaps have sex with, it is tremendously liberating. Here each of us is free to be free, if only for the evening."

Pausing for the effect, Robert continued, "Typically men have more jealousy issues than women. It probably has something to do with our 'possessive gene.' We men tend to think of our women as ours when in reality they are each their own person, and we have no more right to possess them than does a stranger on the street. Normally, we create a strong bond with our women by friendship, relationships, engagement, marriage or lifelong commitments to care for and protect them, that's partly why we think we own them. We also do that here, we care for and protect our partners in this activity we call swinging, but we don't 'own' them. I can't stress that enough and the longer you are in the lifestyle the more you will understand the special bond between us, those of us here, others we meet in the lifestyle and even lifestyle people across the country we may come in contact with. Lifestyle members are a large community in this country and the world. Swinging exists nearly everywhere, the customs are different, but basically all swingers are protective of all other swingers, at least in closed groups like ours.

How are we doing, any questions so far?

Anybody? Yes Scott." He shifted his broad shoulders, leaning forward, almost conspiratorially.

"I hate to bring it up, this has been so much fun but, what about STD's? Amanda and I have been married for nine years now, we're healthy in every respect and I certainly don't want to bring anything into our bedroom that could hurt either of us."

"Good question, Scott. STD's are a concern, but you have provided part of the answer in your question. You and Amanda have a long enough sexual relationship without incident to know you probably do not have any STD's. Also, you are mature enough and concerned about your health that you probably see a doctor regularly for a physical and to check up on any condition that arises Therefore, the rest of us are safe to assume you are free of STD's. Most swingers come from life situations similar to yours. Not all are married, for a variety of reasons, but all are in committed relationships that are disease free. When some problems crop up, STD or otherwise, we take care of it. That's who swingers are; responsible people, like you and me."

Angelea spoke up, "Sometimes, for whatever reason, you will encounter people, males or females, who insist on using a condom for protection. That is perfectly fine, it's a personal choice, and we all respect that. Likewise we all respect the choice anyone can make by declining to 'party' with another member. A simple 'no thank you' or 'not just now' means 'no.'

She continued, "We do recommend that you get checked for any, repeat any, communicable disease prior to participating, and not just a sexually transmitted one. Its just good sense to have a 'baseline' before you start something new. You maybe got a blood test before you were married, it's even required in some states. If you feel uncomfortable going to your family doctor, we have located a walk-in clinic that will do a completely anonymous STD check for sixty dollars. There is a stack of their cards on the hall table, take one if you like. Also, if you are carrying around a head cold, the flu or any other common communicable malady, please stay home. Skip the party that week, we don't want your flu bugs."

Robert picked up there, "Speaking of parties, usually Angelea and I host a party here at our house twice a month on the second and fourth Saturday of the month. Occasionally, if it is a long month or the dates align with a long "dry" spell between parties, we'll have a "bonus" party, to fill in the gap, we'll let you know. Sometimes we don't have a scheduled party due to family commitments or other reasons. Parties start at 7pm, you are welcome any time from then until 9pm when the doors are closed and locked. You may leave at any time, but you cannot return once you walk out the door. Don't bring any "guests" with you without our prior permission. You all are here today because someone, already a member, is recommending you. They gave Angelea your name and number and we make the call inviting you to this seminar. This is the only way anyone is invited in . . . the only way. Angelea and I are a private couple hosting friends in our home, period. We decide who comes and who stays, but, (with a big smile) we try to be nice about it! We've done this before and are pretty good at selecting people who will fit into the lifestyle, although we do sometimes make mistakes, we try to correct them as soon as possible. Please don't be nervous, we are fair, just selective about who we want our friends to be, you probably do the same when you meet new people."

Angelea spoke up, "We will wind up here about 3:30 or 4 o'clock and I will call you this afternoon with an invitation or not. If yes, you will be invited to join us at no charge as guests for a party tonight beginning at seven, as Robert said. When you get here we will introduce you to a host couple that will be your guides for tonight and introduce you to other members who may come tonight. We never have an exact list of who's coming, but from what I've heard we may have about fifteen couples, one single guy and two single gals, members whose spouses are no longer with us. We are like family here and we don't forget those in circumstances not of their making, single people need love too.

I'll tell you now what to bring and what to expect just to save time on the phone. Things get hectic around here on party nights, especially when we have a seminar beforehand . . . Ok, what to wear; wear any street clothes to get here. At about nine o'clock we 'dress down' for the evening, women bring something that you feel comfortable in, sexy is great; just don't come in jeans and an old sweatshirt, who would want to dance with someone like that? Some women simply bring a sari or wrap and wear it stylishly. Pareau, a Tahiti wrap is also popular. Some nudity or peek-a-boo clothes for dressing down is fine, just not full nude please, as we will be gathering back in this room or around the pool when not partying with someone."

"Doesn't that sound like fun?" she said with an infectious laugh.

"Men, for dressing down; shorts, gym shorts, T shirt or not, something to sit on. We follow the same rules as nudists, sit on a towel or have clothes between you and what you are lounging on. We have one member who favors Pareau's as well, he laments the passing of kilts, thinks they're much more suited to what we do here. It's also convenient if you bring a small gym bag for your street clothes, that way they don't get lost, or get inadvertently worn away by someone else.

Bathing suits are certainly permitted, but rarely used. The pool area is completely private and nude swimming is a great way to get acquainted-up close and personal. The hot tub is the great ice breaker for you and your new friend but please, no sex in the hot tub, the pool is ok for those so inclined. There is an outdoor shower on the wall behind the pool, feel free to use it anytime, before or after sex, bathrooms also have showers and a supply of towels, washcloths and soap. Please use but don't waste. Put used towels in the hampers nearby.

This brings up costs. We do not sell anything but we have to charge a fee for parties, currently $50 a couple for each party, after your first free party. This money is used for the midnight buffet, which will be similar to what you just experienced. All soft drinks are free as are hors d'oeuvres and snacks all evening. It also pays for laundering all the towels and sheets, consumable supplies, replacements, etc. We also pay a person to come in the following day to launder everything and clean the house thoroughly. There will be a door person at the front door when you come in. Please have a check made out to Tropical Palms for $50, or cash. We simply don't want to bother with credit cards, and who wants a paper trail there anyway.

Tropical Palms is a non-profit social club with a business license from the city, which allows us up to 50 people for an event, here in our home. We like and respect our neighbors, many of whom are straight friends, so please be careful and park in designated spots, not on their lawns.

What else to bring . . . not much. A good friendly attitude will help you make many friends and contribute to your having a really good time. If you want booze, bring your own, there is a bar in the kitchen. Put your name on your bottle and take it home with you if you want the remainder. Anyone making an ass of themselves by drinking too much will be asked to leave pronto! Twice and you won't be back . . . I hope I haven't dampened your expectations too much. Robert do you have anything to add?"

"Sweetheart you've covered it all very well. There are some pesky details we require of all guests before they become members and attend parties. Here is a copy of the Privacy Agreement for each of you. We ask you to read and sign it before you can attend any party. We would also like to make a copy of your driver's license just to verify your age and identity. These documents are safe with us, used only to insure we are all in the same place, and to keep us safe from prying eyes."

Angelea went off to their home office to make copies of driver's licenses while Robert handed out Privacy Agreements and pens. Everyone read and signed the simple agreement except Burt and Betty who said they would think about it. Angelea returned with the licenses and picked up the privacy papers, Robert left us with one last comment,

"There is just one thing I'd like to remind everyone of something we covered earlier. This is a 'no pressure' zone. If you want to party with someone and they say no, or no thank you, or not just now, don't pester them. We believe in the rule of no, no is always no. Your time will come if you are nice, pleasant and they are attracted to you.

As everybody started to leave, there was a spontaneous hug between Amy and Heather. They had come to this together and now felt a connection way beyond their previous friendship. Wendy gave them both a hug while their husbands shook hands or slapped one another on the shoulder. Wendy's eyes said she wanted to give Kevin a big hug then and there but decided it was possibly not yet time to make such a move, "*Later,*" she thought, "*Maybe tonight?*"

Angelea stood by the door and just hugged everyone! It was her nature and none could resist a slight or enthusiastic hug back. Robert wished everyone a safe ride home with a big smile.

After they all left it was like all the air had gone out of the room, Robert collapsed into the big double recliner and pulled Angelea in with him.

"What do you think, did we get some good prospects today?" he said, giving her a kiss and long hug.

Kissing him back she held the hug, "I think so, I liked them all except that skinhead with the skinny wife," she giggled. "I can't help the skin thing, hair is so attractive on a man and to simply shave it off . . . plus I think he pushed his wife into coming and she wasn't buying. Where did they come from, anyway?"

"He's done some construction work for Frank and Amber at their cabin and commented on their hot tub, about wanting to be naked in the woods, that sort of thing. So Frank thought they might fit, but he's never met the wife."

"Well, I'd like to invite the rest but hold back on them, at least for now. I just didn't hear her say anything more than hello or thank you."

"That's ok by me, I'd better get started prepping the rooms, if you'll make the calls. Jerry and Sharon are our seconds tonight, and they'll be here about six. I don't know who's working the driveway parking, maybe Jerry knows."

The doorbell rang. As Robert got up to answer the door Angelea said, "I think I'll call Rose to see if she can help out, it looks like we'll be having a great house party tonight."

It was the caterer with their midnight supper in cartons. The neighbor across the street waved.

THE GREEN DOOR

"AMY AND KEVIN, we are delighted to invite you both to attend the party this evening, as our guests, beginning about seven." Angelea called Amy just as she and Kevin walked in the door. Kevin had not yet moved in with Amy although they were talking about it, there were family problems to overcome; her kids, her ex, her ex's parents . . . many problems.

"Hold on Kev, it's Angelea," she motioned him on in, a smile spreading across her face, "Yes, thank you Angelea we enjoyed it very much, Kev and I would be delighted to come tonight, we are really looking forward to it and meeting some of your, ah . . . friends! Yes and yes, thanks again, see you soon, bye."

"Well, that was quick." She said, letting the implications of the phone call sink in. She and Kevin were going together, as a couple, to a swing club tonight! It wasn't the same as an engagement, it wasn't being married, but it was some recognition that they were a "committed couple!" That was something to build on.

She trembled with excitement, so much had happened since her divorce, so many new things, new people, new ideas giving her a whole new outlook on life. Was this the way life was supposed to be? It sure seemed a better way than before . . . there just weren't words to describe how she felt, Oh-o-o-o-o-o!

"Go Kev, go. I've got to get ready—you do too, and I've got to call Heath, to see if they got "the call." God I hope so, I need her moral support tonight more than ever, bye now, scoot-see you soon lover!" With that she plunged headlong into the dressing issue, what to wear, what to take and getting the body beautiful for tonight . . . Amy had to call Heather for the first of many calls about her anticipation and just what to wear. The scene in both bathrooms that evening was both electric and hectic. Fortunately this was her ex's week to parent the kids so Jessie and Jimmy were over at his house or their Grammy's house and Amy was free to dash around the house wearing nothing but her fantasies running wild. Her phone, almost continually tied up with calls either to or from Heather and one or two to Kevin until they got the evening dress code sorted out.

The meaning of "guests" was that there was no charge for this first time and that it was a trial period to see if they enjoyed themselves and if others liked having them there. There was one other unspoken requirement, which Angelea had not mentioned in the phone call; it was that both Kevin and Amy would experience another partner that evening, not together as a couple, but individually, with another person. While Angelea and Robert would make sure some of the experienced members would be available for them each to experience another person sexually. No one would actually arrange a date for them, they would have to ask or accept another person on their own. Actually as newbie's they would be in demand from the other experienced members but the two new couples would have to participate and not just come to watch the "action." As Robert would stress in later discussions, it was important to fully participate, no sideliners or party dates.

So in their respective bathrooms they were showering, shaving (both of them) trimming, and primping in anticipation of what was to come, and since they didn't know exactly what the evening would entail their imaginations were running like lottery numbers bouncing in a cage, imagining what their "dates" might be like tonight. Amy called Heather again and again for girl advice but was left without much more than her own gut feelings. Both girls were so excited there was more nervous laughing than real talk. Somehow they got it together.

Jeff and Kevin were left on their own pondering what they should wear for dress down, but being guys they couldn't ask anyone for advice. Shorts obviously, but what kind, that old speedo bathing suit was a little too racy. In the end Kevin went for some sailing shorts that were a little too tight but looked cool with leather patches on the seat and a regatta T-shirt. For Jeff it was harder to look cool, his clothes were more on the banker side than the boxer. Ultimately he threw in just a pair of tennis shorts and a logo "T" into his newer gym bag, they would have to do.

The girls tried on and changed their costumes several times requiring several phone calls before basically deciding to go with what they'd started with, a sari with gold lace trim for Amy and for Heather a summer sheath dress with strategically placed openings showing a bit of boob and a lot of thigh. They each took their own car in case one couple wanted to leave earlier than the other.

All over town a similar situation was playing out with other couples who were attending tonight. The protocol was that "regulars" who came to every party without fail were known and did not need to notify Robert & Angelea. Others, who attended only occasionally or who were fairly new, would call first to be added to the party list for the evening. Guests were those who were attending for the first or second times after attending an orientation earlier. Robert entered all the names on his laptop and he would run off a guest list and print nametags for whoever was manning the front door to give out as people arrived.

Nametags for the newbies came with a light blue border, making it easier to help the new people be identified. Regular member tags had no border. Even some of the regulars needed their memory prompted after having missed a few parties. Tags just made it easier for everyone to circulate and chat with friends until 9:pm when street clothes were replaced with "dress down" party clothes and all the nametags came off. Angelea had called Julie earlier.

"Julie could you and Mark come by a little early and help them through the first few minutes of their first party, get them introduced around, you know."

"No problem," Julie was delighted and looked forward to seeing the two women again and their mates. She even felt a little pride in her introduction of new people to the wonderful world of swinging, that "missionary thing."

Jerry and Sharon, helpers for the evening, arrived about 6:30 and after dropping Sharon at the front door, Jerry drove on to the vacant lot and parked their car. Inside the house minor chaos reigned as the excitement grew by the minute. Word spread there would be three new couples at tonight's party, and that alone was enough to crank up the anticipation level and draw out more couples who might have been on the fence about coming to tonight's party. New people were always an attraction.

Rose was setting up the hors d'oeuvres on the dining table; Angelea and Robert were stocking bathrooms and bedrooms with towels, and washcloths. Robert turned on soft lighting and cued up music on the whole-house sound system. His stack of cd's for making love could run for days without a repeat.

Rose made a final check of bathrooms and then finished arranging flowers on the dining room table and gave thumbs up to Robert as he swept into the room, checking on everything. Parties always made him happy. Catching her hand, he gave her a quick kiss, and danced with her on a short, little routine around the dining table. Being with true, loving friends was truly a blessing for both of them.

Rose had lost her husband to a rapidly evolving melanoma a couple of years before, at far too young an age. As a couple they'd helped Robert and Angelea with the formation of the group in the beginning and it was only natural that she became an extension of their family when he died. They tried to help her cope and she helped them manage the party details. Often she stayed for the parties, enjoying herself with some of the partners she knew when her husband was alive and that was ok, for most of the women accepted her as their equal. In return for helping out, she was not charged the party fee and an occasional $50 found it's way into her pocket after a particular heavy night following the cleanup.

There was also a circumspect cleaning lady who came the following day to launder and put away all the linens, cleaning the house thoroughly. Two days following the parties, there was no indication that anything unusual had happened in this home of two active semi-retired persons. Even the neighbor on one side of the empty lot praised Robert (Bob he called him) to other neighbors for keeping that vacant lot mowed.

Promptly at seven o'clock some of the regulars began arriving at the Green Door to be greeted by Angelea or Sharon. The regulars all knew where to stash their bags of dress down clothes and quickly began their rounds of greeting fellow (and gal) members. The greetings and gossip quickly overwhelmed the background music, as the party got livelier by the minute.

Adam and Wendy arrived early, anxious to meet and greet everyone in their new Palms family. In the other club they'd heard stories, and tonight was their night to separate fact from fancy. Walking through the living room, Wendy immediately recognized two couples from other swing parties and peeled off to visit with them. Jerry and Adam started comparing notes about this and other clubs and were soon deep into the common ground of swinging. By eight o'clock most members and guests were circulating; chatting, noshing the hors d'oeuvres, meeting people and getting up to speed. Wendy quickly made two dates for after dress down. She was excited, glowing and very happy with this new group of people. She loved the lifestyle and wanted to "do" as many good men as she could at parties and here was a room full of new stock. Jerry and Adam decided to find the other new guys and make sure they were mingling ok. Jeff was at the hors d'oeuvres filling his plate when Adam found him,

"Hi, remember me from this afternoon, I'm Adam. Oh, I forgot, I guess you can read my name tag, right?"

"Hi Adam . . . Jeff."

"Jeff, this is Jerry, they're friends with Robert and Angelea."

Jeff sat his plate down and extended his hand, "Glad to meet you Jerry."

"Did you come through the orientation today?"

"First time, learned a lot I didn't know."

"That's what we all find . . . this is a whole different world existing right under our feet, or next door, depending on where you live," Jerry said laughing.

"What are you delinquents going on about . . . whatever it is I'll bet it's nasty," Sharon sidled up to Jerry, "And who are your new found friends?"

"Honey, come meet Jeff. He and Heather came through the seminar today with Adam and his wife Wendy. That's her over there surrounded by all those horny bastards trying to score a date," nodding toward Wendy, who was the center of attention and loving it.

"I know, I was there a few minutes ago and I think she already has her entire evening booked."

"She doesn't waste time," Adam observed, "Strike like a shark in a pool of guppies is her philosophy, she does like her men and she's going to get some tonight."

"Whoa, then I'm wasting time here, I'd better get over there before her dance card is full," Jerry said, "Will you excuse me?"

"Only for new untried sex," Sharon said, calling out after him, "Try for a threesome Honey, or a pile up later."

"Or a twosome might be nice," Adam said, turning his deep dark eyes on Sharon. She smiled, her eyes flashing back a message of delights to come if only he plays his hand right. Jeff took the hint and faded away, they were pros at this flirting and obviously on a different wavelength. He had a lot to learn he mused to himself. Better get going and learn the ropes, but first "*I must find Heather, to see if she is ok.*"

The noise level truly reached party atmosphere, one needed to practically shout in someone's ear to be heard, which didn't hurt the mingling and touching. Robert's cool rock music, playing a solid bass beat, kept people moving and made it hard not to bounce in time. Out on the patio an impromptu dance party had started with two couples, one of them was Heather with another lady rocking to the music. Jeff joined in and the three of them got to grooving to, "*Oh girls just wanna have fun!*"

Amy and Kevin, the other new couple from today's orientation, were doing ok too. When they arrived in the driveway several of the men were out there to help park Kevin's GLK. Chad opened Amy's door to help her down. Her slinky red dress caught on the seat edge and pulled up nearly to her hips as she slid off the leather seat and almost into his arms. She glanced surprised at Kevin on the other side of the car then quickly back to Chad whose tight jeans stretched over his lean muscular physique, just the way she liked it.

"Hi, I'm Chad. This is my wife Pat." His voice was deep, just the sort of voice to match his thick, black wavy hair. *"Oh yeah, he'll do nicely,"* she thought, flashing him her most seductive smile, the one she'd practiced in the mirror earlier.

"I'm Amy. This is Kevin, my-uh, my friend."

"Welcome Amy, I like to meet and greet new ladies, to make sure they're feeling comfortable the first time here." Chad took her arm as they walked together into the house, Kevin and Pat falling in behind them. Once inside, he found her nametag, pinning it on her. "Is there anything I can do to make you more . . . comfortable, Amy?" He looked right into her eyes, emphasizing the word comfortable with a quirk of one eyebrow.

"Hmmm . . ." And the flirting was on. She swam into his dark velvety eyes, holding the contact much longer than would have been proper in any other circumstance. *"Comfort* is not exactly what I had in mind." *Oh, but this was fun, much better than she'd even imagined.* It just felt so-o right. Not to mention blazingly hot. Her panties went from dry to damp the moment he helped her out of the GLK.

Kevin was completely forgotten as she leaned in, her moist lips mere millimeters from his right ear. "You've already made me comfortable, and a few other things that I'd like to tell you about later."

"Does this mean we have a date?"

"If you are asking . . . yes!"

His voice came from deep within those tight jeans, "I wouldn't have it any other way."

Kevin was a little slow at recognizing what had just happened, realizing that Amy had made a date with Chad in front of him just inside the front door. Though when he did, to his credit he turned a wistful smile on Pat as she pinned his blue edged nametag on,

"I'm new at this," stammering and making like a little boy in Sunday school he blurted out, "but would you—ah like to show me how this works tonight?" He felt he'd made the great leap into this swinging thing.

Pat smiled, both amused and a little wistfully, "I'd love to but not tonight Kevin. My dance card is full, left over from last week." In consolation, she suggested that Kevin approach someone else first, and taking his arm, said, "come on, let's find you a playmate for tonight." (His ears turned red). She walked him around, introducing him to individual women as they circulated, hoping he would click with one of them (and she could lose him). Pat knew it was easy for some men to attach themselves to one woman and shut out all others simply for convenience or because he might be shy. She then introduced him to several women in the great room and left him in one group of three where it seemed he might fit in. Funny thing, Kevin was usually the life of a party, hitting on all the women in a friendly, non-threatening way and here he was in a pool of women who were all here for the explicit reason of having recreational sex with different men and he stumbled, tongue-tied. It happens.

Julie and Mark arrived late. They'd had an argument about household finances earlier and were hardly speaking when he dropped her at the door and then brushed off the offer from one of the other guys to park his truck. Their tiff had continued when she had tried earlier to hurry him to go pick up their sitter for her daughter Gina. He snapped at her and her hurt lay smoldering just under the surface. Still, she was here to have fun and his attitude notwithstanding, she planned to.

At a quarter to nine Jerry found Robert and told him there were sixteen couples including themselves, one single guy nicknamed, Blind Larry, who was a special case and Rose who was planning to stay for awhile to set up the late night dinner. Robert turned down the music, flashed the lights in the gathering room and asked for a minute or two of quiet. When the roar quieted slightly, he began . . . .

"Thank you all for coming tonight. It's something Angelea and I always look forward to, having our friends in for the evening, it's all of you who make these evenings very special. I hope you have a chance to meet our guests, Amy and Kevin, Heather and Jeff. They were recommended by our own gorgeous "Lady Julie," lets have a round for Julie . . . *applause* . . . and another lifestyle couple is here tonight; Adam and Wendy who some of you may know from other gatherings. If you haven't yet met them, please do so and please show them a . . . good time." He emphasized that last and got agreement from many with Ok's, right-on's and yeas.

"Ok folks, I have just one announcement, the next party on the 21st will be a welcome home for Shawn and April. Some of you may remember them from a couple of years back. Shawn is in the National Guard and his unit was called up to serve. He went to Afghanistan—twice and April moved back East to be near her parents for help with their kids. Well, now he is out of the Guard, twenty-one years serving his country and us. And now they are moving back here . . . to their home and to us. Isn't that wonderful!"

Applause, whistles and shouts . . .

I know you will want to be here to welcome them home in your own special way . . . so we are asking for reservations for this party only. We can legally only accommodate fifty people so the first twenty-five couples we hear from will be invited. Thank you all for being so patient, and waiting so long to get started doing what we do best . . . loving one another. Jerry tells me the doors are locked and the men are loaded, so let's party!"

Almost en masse, everyone in the gathering room sat down their drinks and plates and moved toward the sliding glass doors to the patio and the benches by the hot tub for dressing down. It's odd how people who in one minute can be dressed to the nines discussing lofty things, can then go to dress down and start pulling off their street clothes, passing through the complete nude stage next to a man or woman, doing the same thing with hardly a sidewise glance, well some glances . . . almost all costumes are simple wraps, shorts or dresses easy to step out of later in the private rooms, not even panties or thongs here . . . who needs panties, they just get in the way.

Rose moved around the room with practiced ease, picking up paper plates and utensils then dumping them in the trash bag she'd stashed earlier under the dining room table. After she got most of them bagged, she brought a tray from the kitchen and began picking up drink glasses, taking them to empty in the kitchen sink then straight to the dishwasher. The trash bag went outside to the covered porch where Robert would haul it away tomorrow. He was careful to not bring attention to their house by giving the weekly trash pickup crew anything more than usual household trash from two people. No sense drawing attention to anything. They were doing nothing illegal. Sex between consenting adults is not illegal anywhere in the states, religious bigots notwithstanding, it's guaranteed in the constitution . . . *"life, liberty and the pursuit of happiness."* But, there are nosey do-gooders who sometimes will create a stink where none exists.

Angelea was gorgeous this evening and Robert told her so when she came out to the gathering dressed in a bluish nearly transparent flowing robe showing nothing underneath except her curvaceous body in all it's loveliness. Earlier she had accepted a "party date" with good friend Steven and after dress down, made a point of walking through the great room where the crowd was again gathered, this time in their party clothes. However, as yet, no one was making a move to a room to party with the "dates" they'd made earlier. A sign to begin the evening was desperately needed and Angelea brought it! In her bluish robe she floated over to Steven, gave him a kiss on the cheek,

"Our time has come."

They waltzed down the hall, arm in arm. The ice was broken, the party started. Couples who were just talking, killing time suddenly found it necessary to scoot off in one direction or another, generally in the direction of available rooms. Some opted for the hot tub first and soon it was the center of visible activity, lots of preliminaries taking place there and some good natured jostling to secure the undivided attention of one of the several ladies in the water. Often the hot tub was the first step of seduction, the warm-up-get-naked-together phase, then it was either pool sex or look for a room. Sometimes there was an afterward get-in-the pool-together-to-cool-off-rinse-off phase. After about three quarters of an hour, couples began drifting out of the rooms to the showers, hot tub or back to the pool to cool off and refresh. A few hungry ones found the kitchen and made another drink or nibbled around on leftover hors d'oeuvres.

Meanwhile nothing was happening for Kevin. He did not connect with any of the ladies he had met when Pat introduced him around, he had tried to flirt, yes but somehow couldn't seem to get past the, "Hello, how are you?" small talk with anyone and found himself becoming the "odd man out." There was nothing wrong with him except his mental attitude. Usually, he was the center of attention or if he wasn't, easily made himself so. His job gave him some cachet, people wanted to know him out in the business world. But here he was just a new, unfamiliar face, waiting for what, he did not know. Was he waiting for someone to ask him for sex . . . not going to happen? Was he engaging in stimulating conversation with a variety of people, both male and female, no not yet? What was wrong? He began avoiding groups of people. After all he didn't know them and they didn't know him. He looked for someone he knew . . . anyone. Finally, as the gathering room emptied of everyone except two couples sitting in deep conversation he fled to the kitchen for a drink, embarrassed at his inability to connect with anyone.

Sitting on a stool just nursing a glass of wine, Rose watched him come into the kitchen, head down, not looking at anybody. She'd seen it before. After he poured himself a drink, she said,

"Need someone to talk to?" she asked. The look of terror in his eyes screamed this was the problem. The other part was he wanted to; no he needed to, get laid, and as soon as possible.

"I-I don't seem attractive to anyone," he complained with a hint of whine in his voice, "You-you're Rose, right?"

"That's right, you're new aren't you, what's your name?"

"Kevin."

"And your partner?"

"Amy, . . . this is a mistake, I don't know why I brought her here."

"Kevin, I wouldn't rush to judgment just yet. Sometimes," she said with a knowing smile, "it takes a while to adjust to the freedom this place offers." Then, "Here's another stool, care to join me?

A pregnant pause followed, then he sat down.

"Is she with someone now?"

"Y-Yes, we met him parking our car."

"Was he with a partner?"

"Yeah, uh-huh, Pat or Patricia I think. His name is Chad."

"Oh, I know them well, they're both great people, long standing members here. Don't worry about you wife, Amy is it? She's in good hands, he is a very considerate, very gentle man, a really good choice for her first time in this situation."

That did not sit well with Kevin. After a few seconds of thought he said,

"I don't care how gentle he is, I'm going to get her right now, and take her home." Before he could move, Rose quickly put her hand on his arm.

"Please don't Kevin, your wife will be fine, trust me. I am a woman too and I've been around here since almost the beginning and I've seen this happen many times before. You're angry and hurt by your own perceived failure to score. You didn't worry about your Amy until you were unable to find the right approach to meet a woman here, and ask her to party with you."

He blinked several times staring at her, then, "She not my wife, she's my girlfriend."

Ignoring that, Rose went on, "Let me ask you, did you see any women here you would like to party with tonight?

"W-well sure, of course."

"Then why didn't you ask them? They are all here for the same reason you are, to enjoy sex. We're all here for recreation without guilt, recrimination or consequences. It's like bowling, you go, you play with others and you go home, looking forward to the next time. Can you see it like that?"

"I-I guess I never thought of it that way."

"You went through the orientation today, did you not?"

"Yes."

"Well, I know Robert talked about that, but you were probably daydreaming about having unlimited sex with lots of women and weren't really hearing what he was saying. Is that possible?"

"Y-yes."

"This afternoon, did you think about Amy having sex with another man tonight?"

"Yes . . . but I didn't exactly dwell on it."

"If you were fucking a woman right now, would you be thinking about Amy and another man?"

Her language shocked him, "Well, no I guess, not-no probably not."

"Well then, come on junior, we have a date in the hot tub."

With that Rose got up from her kitchen stool and taking his unresisting arm led him out to the hot tub area, letting him stand there watching as she slowly removed her pull-over dress, then stepped out of a thong and smilingly, helped him out of his shorts before gracefully gliding into the now empty hot tub. The water immediately began it's work on Kevin, relaxing his shoulders which dropped as his body relaxed and he began to lose the tension particularly when Rose slid over and began slowly caressing his thigh. In no time at all Kevin was the raging bull he imagined himself to be. Rose took the hint and quickly steered him out of the hot tub. After drying off, and wrapped only in a towel, they wasted no time and went looking for a bed in an empty room. Finding none, Rose settled on a room with an empty pad on the floor, next to a bed where another couple was vigorously trying to break the house multiple fuck record, pumping and bouncing, kissing and moaning noisily . . . having a great fuck to put it succinctly.

Rose eased herself down on the pad, discarding her towel in the process; smilingly, and with arms and legs open she said,

"Come to me Kevin, do what you want to do, what I want you to do, give me your body." He could not resist—didn't want to and immediately fell into her still wet and warm body. The foreplay that had taken place in the hot tub already prepared them both and Kevin's dick hungrily sought her inner thighs, riding the path to the smooth trimmed lips of her tunnel of love. It took but a moment until his probing cock found her cock pocket, teased it momentarily before plunging into her sweetness full length. The sensation of fucking a new woman was almost more than he could take, leading him to shudder and shake. He tried to concentrate on stroking slowly, savoring the heat and wetness of Rose, so different from Amy yet familiar as if he had been there before. Rose's great experiences with multiple partners prepared her for this and she was no less thrilled with his penetrating, throbbing, loving, than he was. It had also been some time since she enjoyed a lover and she was making the most of it, letting herself go, reaching for that moment of ecstasy when it all came together for her vajizzle. Kevin, building toward his own climax, trying to feel hers and tried to slow down in the moment while he could still exercise some control, trying to match her breathing, heartbeats and thrusts to flower her blooms as her body pushed back and pulled his dick in until they both exploded into the bliss of two lovers uniting, merging, thrusting . . . releasing.

It was lovely, there on the floor pad, hearing the sounds of lovemaking above them so close they could have reached up and touched the other couple. When it was over, lying on the mattress pad Rose hugged Kevin tightly and finally as their breathing returned to near normal whispered in his ear.

"Thank you Kevin, you've made my evening."

"How is that?" Kevin whispered back still breathing hard, "you were the one who grabbed me by the balls and got me out of my funk, I owe you."

"No you don't owe me, we helped each other is the way I see it, being a widow, somewhat of an outsider now I never want any other gal to think I'm having designs on her man. Having you come along needing a push was good for me too, that's why I thank you."

He could accept that. They lay there in each other's arms, neither wanting to break the spell. Finally Rose made moves to wrap up in her towel and leave,

"I've got to set up the midnight supper, would you like to help," she whispered?"

"Sure," he scrambled up wrapping in his towel and followed her out. The couple on the bed started again oblivious to Kevin and Rose, apparently once was not enough for them.

"I need to freshen up first, let me shower and I'll meet you in the kitchen." She stepped into a bathroom and closed the door. Suddenly on his own again and thinking he should do the same, he went over to the outdoor shower. He enjoyed a cool shower, standing nude for anyone to see, gave him some confidence back, he'd just enjoyed sex with a beautiful woman and here he was showering out in public, announcing it to the world. He even enjoyed his still partially engorged penis, showing he was ready for more. Unfortunately there was no one around to see it. Finally, toweling off and retrieving his T-shirt and shorts, he made himself presentable for work in the kitchen with Rose. Suddenly, he remembered Amy,

"Where the hell was she?"

THOSE WHO'D EARLIER made a second date began to circulate, chatting and waiting for their dates to show. When they did, it was time for more preliminaries, flirting and light romancing in public before looking for a room. Jeff anticipated a date with Tina, his earlier dance partner with Heather out on the patio. She had promised him her second date for the evening and he was impatient, and a little apprehensive, following another man with her. Would she be comparing them, would he feel or sense that other man who had her first? Damn, there was a lot to this swinging he'd not thought about. Jeff was Mr. Cool and with this waiting around he definitely felt un-cool.

He was watching others in this gathering come together with a new partner, learning how it was done; even if they were someone you knew well and partied with many times before. It was kinda like meeting your love at a station in a strange city when you had been apart for a long time. There was nearly always a hug or kiss in the public area, just like an airport waiting area, the anticipation, the wondering, first glimpse when your lover comes to you and you leave together, in this case to a hot tub, pool or room to begin the lovemaking. Much quicker and more satisfying than meeting your lover in the airport. The atmosphere in the great room stayed electric, but not so hectic, the initial ardor having cooled somewhat and new lovers were taking it slower now, but perhaps loving it better. Having released their initial pent up energy they could afford, or wanted to, slow it down and enjoy more. Jeff resolved to relax and meet some new people, he was going to 'fit in', that was something he did.

Rose, in the kitchen, was beaming. She'd done a good turn getting Kevin "broken in" and now she would also have some help setting up the late night repast. Together they pulled the caterer's boxes out of the double Zero refrigerator. She got platters out of the tall kitchen cabinets and started arranging the sandwiches and finger food on the trays then Kevin carried them out to the dining room with Rose right behind him arranging the table. She knew there would be a lot of hungry people tonight, the lovemaking was going well. One could tell by the lack of people in the great room and also the undercurrent vibes resonating throughout the house were heavy with good sex. Kevin kept busy, and for a few minutes while he was still basking in the glow of his recent lovemaking with Rose, his mind stayed away from the big question.

"Where was Amy?"

In the great room, couples returning from their lovemaking began gathering again, exchanging smiles, knowing glances and hugs, those so inclined were scouting around for their next party. Others were resting from their labors on the leather sofas and hassocks. Those serious about lining up second round dates were up and about.

Chad and Amy came out from their party and joined the group of six or seven hanging out in the shallow end of the pool, some in a loose group hug and others quietly getting connected and making slow loving moves surrounded by their friends, who sometimes touched and stroked the lovemaking couple as one would stroke a favorite puppy. It was all new and very heady to Amy, who as an Army brat growing up never felt so much love from so many. It was not long until Chad, mirroring her feelings, began to be aroused and they slipped together again without much effort, she, riding gently in his saddle with his fuck stick firmly holding her in place. She didn't know it then, but she'd found a regular, someone who, in the future would look for her at almost every party, they would have an unspoken standing date and he would look after her and be an understanding male friend when she needed one. Eventually, they slipped apart as hunger took sway over desire they got out of the pool, toweled off, and dressed again in their party clothes. Chad held her hand as they walked back to the great room, letting go only when she spotted Kevin in the dining room. Coming up behind him she gave him a squeeze. He knew that hug and his face brightened tremendously.

"Hey lover, can we have a date?"

"Oh . . . sweetheart, there you are. I've been worried, didn't see you all evening." Kevin gushed, turning around to give her a proper hug.

"I missed you, where have you been?"

"I was with Chad, don't you remember, he and Pat were at the door when we came in. He sort of showed me around giving me the scoop on the different rooms set up for partying, and then we went to the hot tub for a few minutes to "loosen up" as he says. He was right, the hot tub really works, it releases all sorts of inhibitions. It wasn't until then that he actually asked me if I'd like to party with him. He said he would take it slow and go no further than I felt comfortable. He was so nice, I was in control the whole time, I like this kind of loving. It seems so . . . I don't know . . . natural, the way we human beings are supposed to be, don't you think?"

"I-I guess so, I just missed you that's all. I guess I got a little worried when I didn't see you."

"But, didn't you party with anyone?" Amy asked glancing at Rose, sensing some connection from the easy way he was helping her set up the buffet.

"Y-yes," he was still hesitant about this free and easy sex, this admitting in front of his new girlfriend that he just had sex with another woman, and practically under her nose. It seemed like the greatest thing in the world when they were in the orientation, but pulling it off was something else. He thought of Amy and then thinking of Rose got a nice warm feeling from that also. She rescued him and he appreciated it. It was so confusing, not at all like a swing party in his imagination. Being here was just like any other party gathering, except half the people you saw were nude, or making out or both. It was an awful lot to take in, all in one night.

"So who's with this handsome guy?" She said, putting her hand on Kevin's shoulder and looking at Amy, I'm Rose."

"Hi Rose, thank you for looking after my man tonight," Amy smiled at Rose and touched her arm. She thought about giving Rose a hug but held back, not yet sure of all the social niceties of this party.

"No problem, he didn't need much looking after, just a friendly ear and a pat on the butt. This place can be pretty intimidating to the uninitiated, but then I've been here since day one so I can't really judge. Excuse me, I still have some food in the kitchen that needs to be out here on the table."

"Can we help?" Amy asked. "No, I've got it, thanks anyway."

Just then Jeff and Heather came arm in arm into the dining room excited to tell of their evening so far, joining Amy and Kevin. They had passed the unwritten test, each finding someone to break the ice with and join the insiders. Across the table, a slight dishwater blonde girl in a short baby doll night dress was picking at the food smiling at Jeff who kept smiling back but didn't leave Heather's side. She wandered away. Rose came in with another tray and, putting it down, came over to Kevin and the group.

"If you like let me introduce you around to some of our friends," she broke into a clique of three women in animated conversation nearby.

"Girls, this is Kevin, Amy, Heather and Jeff. All new fodder for your gossip mill . . . just kidding of course."

"Pay no attention to Rose," one of the ladies said, "she's just jealous because we don't talk about her as much as the other Mary Jane's, isn't that right Rosebud. I bet she didn't tell you her nickname either did she?"

Amy, playing the dumb blond asked, "You mean like Citizen Kane's Rosebud?"

"No, more like the flower where the sun don't shine," answered Susan who started the joke.

"You all are so cruel," Amy said laughing, stretching out the c-r-u-e-l.

"No sweetheart, not cruel, just bitchy because Rose gets her pick of the men here while we have to take the same one home every night. Anyway, don't mind me, welcome to the Palms family, in spite of what we say, we're good friends and welcome you into our sin city, I'm Susan, this is Tina and Dawn, say hello girls."

"Yes to that, hello," Tina spoke up. "I would introduce my husband Greg who was just here a minute ago but now he is over there trying to seduce Angelea again. He keeps trying but she is very selective and so far, he hasn't made the cut."

"Well I guess you can't fault him for trying, huh?"

"No Heather, but he just doesn't seem to know when it's a lost cause."

Jeff kept his eye on Susan and when he saw the group breaking up, said,

"Hey Susan, can we talk?"

"Hi, sure, Jeff is that right? Enjoying yourself are you, is this is your first night?"

"Well, yes Susan, yes and yes, but I think I'd enjoy it more if we could spend some time together. Can I buy you a drink and find a seat to talk."

"Lead on O'fearless leader," they went to the kitchen and the bar. Jeff was learning the women here were truly liberated; they were what made the parties work, and heaven help the man who forgot it. With a bottle of Fiji water they went back to the great room, finding a seat on one of the modular leather sofas. Jeff noticed all of the sofas were real leather, nice. Settling down into a pile of pillows, Susan let her sarong fall off her thigh almost to her crotch, seeming not to notice. Jeff eased down comfortably beside her, his free hand resting on her shoulder.

"So Susan, tell me what I need to know to make it here."

"You are doing pretty good so far . . . touching is good," she said wriggling so her shoulder fell further under his touch and putting her hand on his bare leg below his shorts. The reaction to his dick was immediate and obvious.

"Easy boy," she smiled a wide Southern smile, "Save it for later." Embarrassed, his erection softened but his heart was still racing. He felt like a schoolboy again on his first date. Screwing up his courage, he told her so. She was flattered and moved her hand up and patted his crotch.

"Good boy," she said and snuggled further into the pillows, "So Jeff, what would like to do here on your first date that you don't do at home," she asked with an impish grin.

"Oh gosh, I don't know what to say," explaining to Susan, "Heather and I have been together nearly five years now, married two and I suppose we're beginning to cool off a little from the first couple of years."

"I have to admit," he went on, exclaiming, "In the beginning we went at it like rabbits, and we still have sex four or five times a week, but it's not like every morning, noon and night like when we first started living together. Getting married was a good thing, but I miss the hot and heavy sex from . . . earlier . . . when we first got together."

She smiled, nodding agreement.

"Gee, am I spilling too much?" He stammered. Telling Susan all this seemed like a confession or perhaps bragging, he wasn't sure which.

"No, you are doing just fine, we've all been there . . . where you are. That's one thing we like about the Palms," Susan agreed, "Each time we are with a new person, like you for instance, it's like the very first time—again and again."

He couldn't agree more. She smiled an impish grin, emboldening him.

Hesitating, but finally it came out,

"Would you like to make love for the first time again, with me?"

He couldn't believe he just said that, but before he could retract it, she was up off the sofa and taking him by the hand led them down the hall where a couple was coming out of a room,

"Can we continue where you left off?" she asked them . . ."Sure, the room's empty, waiting for you."

Going in, there was a modern king size bed with a canopy, not one of those traditional, frilly things one finds in historic houses but a cool, dark wood framed canopy bed, *neat* he thought.

"This is my favorite room, Jeff, you'll like it here," which further confused him. Did that mean she fucked anybody and everybody in this room. Did it have a lot of history for her? What happened to "the first time?" Was he ready for this? What was he supposed to do?

The room was small with a tall ceiling and was sparsely furnished with cool, modern, clean lined furniture. A valance above the headboard emitted a soft, blue glow, bathing the sheets in a cool aura effect. The previous occupants, the couple they met coming out, straightened the sheets and placed a pair of towels on the foot of the bed. One could hardly tell anyone had been there, much less probably having hot, vigorous sex just moments before. His excitement grew.

Moving slowly, Susan removed his T-shirt then teased her fingers over his chest, swirling around his nips a second or two, too long, they began to rise . . . then she unbuttoned his shorts so her hand could slide down into the fur above his junk, and then cupping his growing cock and balls, which felt like anything but junk, she squeezed gently, lovingly and then stretched up to kiss him full on the lips. He shuddered, feeling cold for a moment followed by a . . . heat flash? Hard for him to tell, she didn't seem to notice and continued feeling him and kissing him until he helped her to get him out of his shorts, letting his now magnificent badboy stand proud and breathe.

She knelt, slowly, keeping one hand on his cock, and with the other hand, traced a sinewy line from his mouth to his cock which she then presented to her mouth, saturating it with her saliva, slipping it in and out of her warm, wet mouth, all the while licking with her tongue, curling around his helmet, teasing under the lip, around the edge, then taking him all down her throat until her teeth tangled in his bush, once . . . twice and once more. He couldn't believe it . . . just couldn't, this beautiful woman he only met a few moments ago now was sucking his cock down her throat.

Releasing him, she motioned to the bed and as he stretched out, in a practiced motion she climbed on the bed, straddling him, and slowly lowered herself, slipping his cock into her vadge—slowly, as if it were the very first time for her.

His heart, pounding out of his chest, waves of pleasure rushing over and over, fighting himself to hold back, to keep from involuntarily thrusting into her as far as he could go and from letting go. She took him all in, a feat Heather sometimes couldn't or wouldn't do. At that moment Jeff knew his was the biggest cock in the world fucking the world's greatest hot pocket! No doubt about it. She kept sucking him in, further and further, where would it stop, where could it stop? Susan supported herself on her knees and began to slowly work her pelvis back and forth, side to side, squeezing and releasing her Kegel muscles, milking his penis from the base to the head. She kept fantastic control, just enough to drive him towards release, but he fought back, not quite letting go, not quite ready and she knew. She stopped very slowly and released him long enough to lay down alongside, kissing and touching, her hand to his balls and the tops of his thighs. He cupped those perfect breasts with tiny nipples, hard and erect reaching for his lips which gratefully found them and began slow, tonguing, sucking, caressing so that now Susan began gasping for breath.

Jeff suddenly needed to be inside her again, his penis ramming the air looking for a home. Moving over her, as gently as possible given the heat, he parted her legs and dropped his mouth to her love nest, just below her curly blonde fuzz. He loved her lickory, lovely lips and pushed aside every fold, opening every recess he could find with his probing and pushing, tingling tongue. When he felt he had explored every dish in the buffet, he lifted and slowly settled inside again, all the way past her inner and outer folds of her vadge, to the dark only a man could find and explore.

Susan's pleasure bucked and shuddered as Jeff came in to home, pulling back, knocked at her door and entered again. Each thrust, each new crash against the gates of extreme pleasure . . . heavenly. Each time he went deep, his penis felt her cherry as he pushed up to her inner sanctum. Women's anatomy was such a mystery, how it could feel so good to his ace in the hole and still be so mysterious, he didn't know and would never learn. But that did not stop him from riding over her hill muffin, holding his own explosion in check until he could feel and hear from her muffled sobs that she was about ready to come with him. She moistened two of her fingers and rubbed her mound faster and harder, just above Jeff's bad boy sliding in and out, in time with his thrusts . . . .

"Yes! Yes! Yes! Only partially smothered screams escaped and her free hand clawed at his arms and shoulders as he rode her from the darkness exploding into the light. His body trying with all it's might to flood her vage with milk and honey. But not quite . . . they almost came together . . . close enough for their first time. In the dim recess of his memory it seemed better than most attempts he'd made to time his climax with Heather's, she was always a little behind him, if she got there at all. Here, in this wonderful blue room with Susan, it felt like they'd flown off a cliff together into a cloud of light. Fantastic! All tension and anticipation coming here tonight totally flashed away. Grateful beyond belief for Susan, her ministrations and for her . . . body!

They lay exhausted, together, neither able to speak and not wanting to break the light show they felt rippling around them. Gradually, without conscious thought, he wanted Heather there with them, he wanted to share with her the pleasure he just experienced, wanted her to feel the high, to feel the love he shared with Susan. What was this, what did it mean? Why was he feeling the need to share this moment with Heather? Would Susan feel the same to him with Heather in bed with them? Then another thought struck. What about Susan's husband (he'd forgotten his name) would he want him there with them . . . this swinging was so confusing. Susan, however, was having no problems with the situation as she shifted position to lay in the crook of his arm, "Mm-m-m that was so nice," Susan murmured, "Your wife is so lucky to have a good (she emphasized the good) man like you, I want to be her best friend and just hope she will share you with me again, occasionally."

Jeff didn't know what to say, he was flattered and more than just a little confused. How was he supposed to keep his emotions in check after wild, exploding sex with a perfect stranger who suddenly was changing his thinking in just a short time? But, he couldn't hold any questions for now, his thoughts simply dissolved, he was too exhausted, and he could only enjoy the feelings, the connection and the warm, loving body next to his.

After a few minutes Susan interrupted his dreaming, "I wonder if we should vacate and give this loving room to somebody else?" With a shock Jeff realized it was over. They separated. He retrieved his shorts and T-shirt from the floor. As he was pulling them on, Susan smoothed the bed, tucking the sheets back in again, "good as new," she whispered and taking his hand, they went down the hall back into reality. He wasn't entirely sure he was ready to leave this fantasy room and Susan, but he followed her, a puppy on her leash.

Back in the great room, now almost empty, Jeff looked for Heather in vain. She was not there. Out in the pool area some people were laughing and one of them sounded familiar. He thought he saw Heather and Amy. Going closer, he recognized Amy with another couple and while the girl resembled Heather's blonde mane from the back, it was not her. It's hard to sort out people when everyone is nude. He did recognize the guy from the group hanging out in the kitchen earlier. Amy turned, saw him and waved.

"Hi Jeff, come meet some new friends, Jim and Kim . . . Kimberly," she corrected herself.

"Hi guys . . . Jim, I remember you from earlier in the kitchen and I'm No-Name Jeff, no name tag now, remember?"

"Welcome to our pool, come in and make us want to want you" Kim said waving her free hand and big smile on her face.

"Sure, come in, join our little floating feel-it-up island," Jim said, waving him toward the steps. Not having anywhere else to go and embarrassed at being caught just staring, Jeff peeled off his shirt and shorts and put them on a nearby chair then walked a little self-consciously to the steps and waded in. Shedding his clothes in front of these people he did not know embarrassed him a little, but he was still riding on Susan's cloud, still had his head high in her clouds.

The girls made an opening for him in the circle and soon he was bouncing gently off the bottom in concert with Amy and her new friends. Putting his arm around Amy seemed perfectly natural but she was almost a stranger to him since she was Michelle and Heather's friend and had always been a single woman around him. This was the first time he ever touched her, not to mention her nude body even though he'd seen her sunbathing with the other girls. On the other side Kim, another nude woman, and his third in less than an hour . . . such simple pleasures, but oh it felt so good. His Stanley Power Tool began to grow and he wasn't even plugged in.

Amy chattering away told Jeff that, "Jim and Kim have a home based business and can work there nude most of the time." He felt Kim's leg against his and further up, his hip grazing hers.

"Yeah, a week not too long ago we decided to try and live the whole week, day and night in the nude . . . well now . . . that's not right, you are either nude or not, you can't be 'in the nude,' there's nothing to be 'in' if you are nude, and well, anyway, we didn't wear anything for a whole week, pulling it off. But on the last day Kim frightened the UPS guy making a delivery."

"It should have been the relief driver, she's hot," Kim said.

"For who, you or me?" Jim wanted to know.

"Either or both maybe," Amy said grinning as she dropped a hand down Jeff's backside, giving his cheek a brush with her hand.

"And that was a busy week, we lost a lot of time making love on the shipping table," Kim laughed.

Jeff responded with his hand on Amy, just grazing across her back. She pinched his butt.

Ouch! Jeff said, "You are a little off there girl, the pump handle is in front!" Jeff couldn't believe he'd just said that to Amy, but there it was. And she was Kevin's girlfriend!

"Really?" She moved her hand around front and he shuddered from her touch—noticing what was happening to Jeff, Kim said, "I want to be naughty with you too," dropping her hand to join Amy. Their murmurings tapered off and stopped as the girls worked together feeling him up, quickly bringing Jeff's cock to attention. After a moment or two of silence from the girls, Jim realized what was going on.

"Hey, me too." Jim pulled his arms around the two girls bringing them close.

"Ah . . . that's it," as they put their other hand to work on him. The group edged their way into shallower water, so they could stand without bouncing. Jim eased Amy to him and started gently rubbing her in the same way she was doing him. It wasn't long until her legs came up and he connected with her underwater, it was so easy and felt so natural to them both, with the water supporting most of their weight, his arms around her neck, slowly bobbing up and down in the water. Amy's face, a dreamy blank spacey look, just enjoying the sensations, not thinking about who her partner was nor where her significant other, Kevin was . . . he was somewhere, could be anywhere, she wasn't thinking of him anyway.

Kim never quite let go of Jeff and now floated around ready to do the same to him. It was a little more difficult; their not having been connected before, it took a few tries to get their bodies to fit together comfortably. Jeff eased Kim over to the sidewall, and supporting himself with one hand on the edge, was able to bring his cock and her now flooded cock socket together in slow harmony. Then a broad smile slowly took over their faces. Pool sex like this could go on and on.

Back in the dining room, activity was picking up around the table, spread with all manner of light snacks. Butterfly shrimp, three kinds of dip, little sandwiches of tuna and chicken salad, and fruit; bananas, chilled apple and pear slices, broccoli and dip, three kinds of salads; loaded potato, veggie and crisp greens. A selection of cheeses and crackers filled out the table. Couples fresh from making love came here to re-nourish their energy while singles grazed the table, looking and being watched by others, sending out vibes asking for their next encounter. One could hang around the table and eventually see nearly everyone at the party, it was a really good meeting place, particularly for the new people who didn't have a roster of regulars, people with whom they partied whenever the opportunity presented.

So, it was only natural that Amy and Kevin would gravitate together to share, and yes, boast some about their evening so far. This coming to the Palms was a big step for them, opening themselves up to loving relationships with others just when they were getting their own relationships going or on solid ground. Amy, satiated from her swimming pool playtime, dried off and dressed again in party clothes. She found Kevin at the table and rejoined him with a kiss and a long, long hug.

"So what do you think about this sweetie?" Amy, still vibrating from pool playtime, had her arms around Kevin, holding him close. "Has our team scored as many points as in the first half?"

"I think it will come out a tie, if you know what I mean. We may need a re-match or go into overtime."

"Can you believe this Julie?" Amy said. "Look at us, a week ago we were blooming innocents."

"Change blooming to fucking and I'd agree with you!" She answered, with a wicked grin.

You know, my history here don't you?"

"No, not really. I know you were married when I first met you at the salon, and then you weren't. But I didn't know why," Amy said. "And I didn't know when you took up with Mark, sorry, I didn't mean it like that, I meant when you and Mark got together."

"It's ok, I understand, I had been coming here with my husband when he split to marry his bosses' secretary, (can you believe that), I wanted to find a way to come back? Being dumped by your husband doesn't qualify you for widow status, like Rose. So one day I got a call from Mark, asking if I would join him to be a couple, just so we could come to these parties again. His GF had dumped him and since we knew each other through the club, I called Angelea to see if we could come back."

"Obviously she said yes, no?"

"She said yes, but we would have to be a committed couple, no other fooling around, it's not safe and Mark and I agreed that's right, I wasn't seeing anyone else anyway, so it was an easy decision and we began coming (giggle) again and sort of just fell into love, Palms love at least."

"That's a lovely story, and a great advertisement for the Palms, right?"

"I guess so, anyway that's how it happened, Mark moved in with me and Gina about six months ago and it seems to be working."

A starving Jeff, coming in for sustenance, joined Amy, Kevin and Julie at the table. Pool play with Kim, and partying with Susan before that had left him wrung out, desperately needing protein. But his Heather was still missing and it began to bother him. Jeff wondered where and who she was with.

"Have any of you guys seen Heather?" he asked, changing the subject. No response from the buffet or any of the hungry nibblers around it. Mark joined the group, going to Julie giving her a perfunctory hug and a kiss before filling his plate. It appeared there was some tension between them tonight, probably because Julie was modeling a very flattering skinny tank top that barely contained her boobs over a short, short mini skirt (with nothing under it), ensuring that eyes followed wherever she went. Tonight, this was beginning to bother Mark. She wasn't exclusively his, but he didn't want to lose her either, so things were not as normal as they might seem in this little Gordian knot of party goers.

Nearing midnight, some couples were saying their good-byes after eating a late supper. Sharon was at the door, giving hugs to men and women alike, some lasting a very long time as she buried her face in their hair, or the curve of their neck, or in long, loving kisses to her friends-with-benefits. Obviously, there was great feeling and much love in this open society of loving people, some even happened to be married to each other. Always helpful, Jerry was out in the driveway assisting people with their cars

Amy and Julie moved from the table after filling their plates and were sitting together on a hassock deep in conversation, talking about kids from the look of it. Nearby, Mark and Kevin found some construction topics that took their interest besides their present common interest, sex and the Palms, and explored them to the best of their natural manly reticence. Jeff hung around the edge of the conversation, not really interested, but having nowhere else to be.

Finally Julie and Amy got up, arm in arm, and with a sparkle in their eyes, announced they were going to the group room, anybody want to join them? There was a pregnant pause until Mark said, "I'll go with you," and broke away from his conversation with Kevin.

"Come on Jeff, you come too, it'll be fun," Amy said, "Julie says you don't have to do anything you don't want to do."

Mark tapped Jeff's shoulder,

"Come on buddy, you need to see this," as he and Kevin followed the girls down the hall.

Jeff declined, "I think I'll pass, I'm going to look for Heather, you all go on."

"Oh no you don't, Jeff you need to see this, even if you don't jump in the dog pile," Mark pushed Jeff out, towards the hallway.

"Ok, but I'm going to look for her first," he wandered down the hall in the opposite direction.

"If you find her, tell her all her girl friends are there," Julie laughed as she flashed her tush and Amy sashayed her sari with the gold trim, as they paraded ahead of the boys down the short hall to the rec room, now outfitted as a group room with wall to wall pads on the floor. The door was open but with dim lighting it was hard to see anything but dark shapes inside. Julie showed them how to enter; get down low and ease quietly into the room, then find a place along the wall or on the mats and sit quietly until someone already there asks you to join them, or gives you a sign to "come in." As Julie and Amy scooted into the room, Kevin and Mark followed, on their knees.

As their eyes adjusted to the dark, they could see one couple at the side making out, and three people, all wrapped up in each other in the center of the room on the mats . . . AND ONE OF THEM WAS HEATHER! That girl learns fast, Julie whispered. After watching a bit Julie caught Heather's eye and both she and Amy moved slowly to the group stretching out on the mats, one on each side alongside Heather, gently touching her. She was being slowly fucked while at the same time playing with another guy's bat and balls kneeling on his haunches up by her head. She motioned to Julie and after caressing her for a few moments with her free hand, moved Julie's hand to the rod she was fondling. Surprised at first, Julie continued slowly caressing the man's cock. He didn't seem to notice the change.

She didn't recognize him but his body was nice and with her ministrations he kept making sexy moans and groans all the while keeping his eyes tightly closed. Julie thought she must be doing something right. Shifting to her knees, she began to kiss and fondle his nips, keeping one hand on his dick, slowly pleasuring him. He moaned louder and began to sway in tune with her hands' motion.

Eventually he opened his eyes, blinking. They were teary from her pleasuring him. Julie and the object of ministrations sat there on their knees for awhile, just drinking each other in as she continued the caressing and he moved a strong, slightly rough hand over her upper body, gently feeling her bosoms and caressing her neck. She looked in his eyes for recognition and realized with a start, that he couldn't see her. He must be blind! She was shocked, not that a blind person could be there, but that she hadn't known earlier. He continued to touch her body, and she realized he was mapping her image in his brain, seeing her body no less than any other man, just doing it by touch instead of eyes.

Julie stretched out on the mat alongside Heather and her blind lover began to lick her pussy, sweeping up and down the length of her vage before tonguing her clit . . . all the while caressing every other part of her body he could reach. Julie dissolved in a haze of pleasure, aware only of incredible touching, tonguing and his low moans of pleasure. Who needs eyes?

Amy went to the other side of the man on top of Heather and began to touch and caress his shaft as he fucked Heather. Then sliding her hand over his buttocks, she encouraged his thrusts. He did not acknowledge her but did not brush her away either and soon Amy, the man and Heather were rocking in unison, touching, caressing, and thrusting as one. Heather's hand also found Amy's cunny, kneading and pulling her pussy in rhythm with the bubba fucking her, Amy's honey soaked Heather's hand, just begging for the two fingers that slid into her vadge along with his dick and brought her to a new high climax there on the group room floor.

Kevin and Mark, still on their knees, sitting on their haunches were fascinated watching the scenes playing out in front of them. Then as their eyes adjusted to the dark found cushions, and leaned them up against the wall and stretched out, watching the lovemaking in front of them, practically at their feet. Their shorts were becoming more and more uncomfortable as they watched. Finally Mark opened his fly, letting his throbbing penis free and absently began to slowly pleasure himself, absorbed in the lovemaking on the cushions just a few feet away.

Another couple came into the room, both of them nude and lay down on the pads beginning the loving cycle at their own speed. Her hair was loose, long almost to her waist and she flung it over both of them like a cape . . . sexy beyond belief, Kevin thought, *"I could do her in a heartbeat,"* The atmosphere in the room grew thick, heavier, with the moans of lovemaking coming from all sides, all around.

 God he wanted a woman, any woman, Amy, or Julie or someone! Kevin could stand it no longer and slipped out of his shorts intending to somehow join Amy, Heather or Julie in the center of the room with his now thoroughly hard cock.

But what was this? A hand on his cock holding him, then slowly sliding up and down, he was nailed to the mat with Mark's rough hand. He wanted to pull away, to slap that hand, to punish it, and move away from Mark, but he couldn't. It felt so good, a strong man's hand on a cock is like no other. A wave of pleasure kept him from resisting, unable to stop himself from his own impulses he reached for and tentatively touched Mark's boner. He hadn't done that since he was a boy, jerking off out in the garage with the neighbor kid. They continued this way for a while, neither looking at the other, being in the dark helped . . . just slowly pleasuring each other, not trying to force the issue. Both men enjoying this little walk on the wild side. The atmosphere in the room, already intense, grew heavier.

Two more women came into the room and finding a spot near the center group, began kissing and fondling each other quietly, adding to the room's electricity. They went at their lovemaking just like a man and woman only there was no man meat involved. Just electrons and passion from vadge to vagine, Ben & Jerry meeting Bob & Ray and a tit for a tat. Fascinated, Kevin watched these two women deeply involved in making their own kind of unselfconscious love. Watching them Mark made no other moves on Kevin, just kept his hand sliding up and down his woodie, while watching the girls in the center of the room, lovingly, almost as if they were loving him.

Julie saw Mark and Kevin pleasuring each other making her want more than just Heather's hand on her. She moved over to reach the boys and gently moving Kevin's hand away from Mark's cock replaced it with her warm, wet mouth, sliding slowly up and down in rhythm to Mark's hand on Kevin. Then moving slightly between them, she mouthed Kevin's cock, slowly sliding down until she swallowed him in a deep throat grip that left him shuddering. Julie quickly returned to Mark and kept the pleasure going with him also. As Julie labored on, the boys became more excited and Kevin slid up tight alongside Julie and was able to touch her pussy, and slip a couple of fingers in while she teased his cock. Empowered by the teasing, Julie intensified her pleasure work sucking each jism cannon in turn until they finally emptied their passion in spasmodic shock waves as each exploded all over themselves . . . it was a mess.

The action in the middle of the room got more intense, drawn on by the moans and groans and shrieks from the side. At this moment Jeff walked in, his stiffly upright presence casting a pall over everything.

"HEATHER!" he cried out, seeing his wife on the floor naked and surrounded by two other naked men, one touching and one fucking her with long, supple, full body thrusts. Jeff moved in to stop that man (she was HIS WIFE now, not Heather). She saw him coming and panicked!

"Jeff, stop . . . Jeff!" Heather screeched, "It's ok hon, it's ok . . . come lay down with me, here." She patted the mat like you would to teach your pet new words. Heather's fucking partner in the dog pile, retreated to the edge of the mat and protested, "I'm sorry, I didn't mean . . . to," and fell silent.

Clearly, Heather was where she wanted to be and would have to work to bring Jeff along with her to the same place. But for now, he was a big-time hurt puppy and needed tender loving care of his own. He lay down alongside her and buried his face in her ample breasts, feeling safe at last. He'd found her and they were safe together, no matter where they found themselves at the moment.

Julie found a pile of fresh towels in the corner and took one for herself and a couple for her friends. Things quieted down while everybody took a deep breath and relaxed a bit, going back to enjoying where they were and who they were with. Kevin and Mark sort of peeled away from each other and Kevin scooted closer to Amy, and they all buried themselves in kisses and loving touches, pushing back out of their consciousness what just happened. But after recovering some in Heather's arms . . . Jeff stiffened, he was having none of it.

"I don't know how you could come in here and fuck around with a bunch of strangers and not let me know," his voice shattering the silence in the room, "I don't know who this person is anyway?"

"Jeff . . . Jeff," Heather purred in a motherly tone, brushing his hair and gazing in his eyes.

"It's ok, it'll be fine, we were just having fun, that's what we're here for isn't it, fun? Besides my friend Julie was here with me, it wasn't going anywhere, we were just playing around . . . I don't even know their names . . . it's just simple sex . . . nobody is supposed to get hurt . . . I don't want you hurt, you do still love me don't you?"

"Heather I . . . I don't know what to say. This is all too new, too confusing for me to handle right now . . . can we just go . . . please? Jeff was having a bad experience. It was a plaintive plea as he sat up and looked around.

Across the room a deep voice said, "Take it outside!"

Meanwhile, Kevin next to Amy was all wrapped up cuddling and caressing. Julie and Mark were getting ready to leave, both thinking questions to ask and answer to themselves. But, the storm had passed.

Julie and Mark went straight to the showers behind the hot tub, showering each other clean of the evening's lovemaking, then after toweling off, retrieved their street clothes and dressed, ready to head home. Julie looking curiously at Mark in a new light after his performance with Kevin.

Jeff and Heather left the group room and went straight to the pool, floating close by each other until their clouds passed and their raging emotions cooled to a steady rhythm. After awhile Amy and Kevin also came to the showers and then dressed to go home. When Jeff and Heather came out of the pool they dressed to go home also. Amy and Kevin sat down at a patio table nearby to wait for Jeff and Heather. Kevin left for a minute, saying, "I want to get something I stashed in the kitchen, I'll be right back."

Shortly he returned with a half bottle of Dom Perignon and four glasses for a toast to cap off their new lifestyle evening.

"I thought Amy and I might have something to celebrate, like an old married couple breaking out and re-kindling the fires, but I never imagined we'd go so far, so fast and with our good friends along for the ride. So this is to celebrate our new outlook on life and more than just friends, we are now lifestyle friends, thanks to you all." he popped the cork and topped up the four Champagne flutes. They sipped the wine each with their own thoughts of what this evening meant to each. It was almost too much to talk about.

Amy asked Kevin, "Do you want to stay longer?" It was really a statement not a question, he shook his head, no, he was ready to go although other people were still milling around, talking and eating the remaining tidbits from the table.

Angelea, at the door gave everybody leaving, long, lovely hugs.

"I can tell you all enjoyed a good time tonight, thank you for coming—and coming! See you again soon. Drive safely going home, we love you."

It was hard to leave. Slowly the four friends walked quietly down the circular driveway. At their car, Heather stopped and gave Amy a big hug.

"Love you, girlfriend," she whispered in Amy's ear, "Call me."

"You too big guy," she mouthed the words to Kevin, then got in their car. Jeff holding the door for her, gave Amy a kiss on the cheek and a hand wave to Kevin,

"See you guys," he whispered, realizing they were in a very quiet, dark neighborhood and it was nearly two in the morning. The two cars slowly made their way down the street and out onto some main roads. Jeff drove slowly to their house about eight blocks away. Neither of them said anything, exhausted from their day, which started earlier before noon. About halfway there Heather slipped her hand on Jeff's leg, giving him a squeeze, just making a connection. In the house they went about their usual bedtime routine and soon were in bed. Despite needing restive sleep, neither could close their eyes, they just lay staring at the ceiling, thinking of the day's activities—all jumbled together.

Suddenly lying there, Heather got a sudden urgent need to hold Jeff very close, and as she turned, he felt the same primal urge and was on her in a flash. They held each other tightly, then tighter still, letting their emotions flow into each other. Heather's mind played back a rush of the evenings activities, meeting Chad and Pat in the driveway as they arrived, the flirting just inside the door and his asking her to be his first date. Her mind wandered back to the group room enjoying two men, not even knowing their names. She thought over her feelings when Jeff found her there, how he was hurt and how she suddenly realized she may have gone too far too fast—without him. A wave of remorse swept over her and she clung even tighter to him, she had a lot to learn about this "swinging."

"I love you," slipped from her lips.

"Oh baby," he shuddered, suddenly aware of his erection and needing to connect, to be in her body, to reclaim the bond they enjoyed. She opened her legs guiding him in, to mother him, and to feel him inside her, coupling, making that connection.

Together they made deep, passionate, euphoric love, bodies and feelings flowing into each other surrounded by a aura never quite experienced before. It was almost like the 'first' time; only they knew each other far better now, a knowing in the biblical sense, as in the mystical joining of two compassionate souls. Neither remembered when it ended, they were fast asleep, exhausted in each other's arms.

6

LINGERING LOVE

ACROSS TOWN, when they got back to Amy's house, she asked him, "Do you want to stay?"
"Sure, yes . . . if it's ok."

Amy and Kevin ran some of the same filmstrips through their memories of the evening, but Kevin was still embarrassed at his inability to connect easily with the women at the party, women also looking for sex. Images of Rose kept running through a warm and hazy, film filter in his muddled mind. Did she really like him or was she just the sag wagon pick-up detail. He also had mixed guilt feelings about his encounter with Mark in the group room. It wasn't just the jacking off with another guy, although the last time he'd done it was as a teenager, no it was a different feeling, a connection with Mark and Julie that was troubling. He liked them both even though he met them for the first time at the party and was confused about his feelings for them, Mark particularly. What does it say about a guy going to a swing party who winds up jacking off with another guy in a group room? What the hell?

Kevin followed Amy into her shower and she made it first to the bed shoehorned into the too small bedroom. She lay there thinking about the evening, hearing the shower running and running, there was a lot to wash off! When he toweled off and got into bed, the light was out and Amy was pretending sleep, turned away from his side. She was not ready to deal with Kevin's erratic behavior. Maybe later, but she did not want to rehash the evening right now, it was too late in several ways. Kevin wanted very much to touch her, to re-connect to the woman he knew before tonight. Tentatively, he touched her shoulder but she didn't respond . . . fast asleep or pretending to be. *"Ok, Leave it for tomorrow,"* he thought.

Next morning, Sunday, Kevin got up about eight, pulled on his sailing shorts from last night then went to the kitchen and started coffee. He padded barefoot out the front door to pick up the paper. He was reading the funnies, drinking his first cup when Amy came paddling out wearing a thin shift, also barefoot. Pushing aside his paper and coffee, without even a "Good Morning" she sat down on his lap draping herself around him and kissed him full on the mouth, then after taking a deep breath kissed him again.

"What brought that on?" He was gently surprised.

"Oh, I just love you this morning."

"More than last night?" He couldn't help asking, remembering her pretending to be asleep.

"I'm sorry, I was exhausted then . . . from the day, the day's events," she added.

"Or more likely the evening's?" He suggested.

"Are you picking a fight?"

"No."

"Sure sounds like it," Amy pouted. "Look, I can't help it if you didn't connect like I did last night. It was just a party and I partied with a couple of more people than you did . . . or one and a half more if you count jacking-off with Mark and Julie."

He flinched, *"That really stung!"*

"Really I don't know what you are so bent about, that's why we went there—to expand our horizons, have a little fun, make new friends . . . did we fuck up?"

He hated her direct, logical analysis of complicated things and he just couldn't answer with her still sitting on his lap, they were too close for words. Sometimes men just have to do what they have to do. Kevin did the manly thing; he picked her up and staggered back to the bedroom. Placing her as gently as he could on the bed shucked his shorts and lay down besides her, just holding her. After a few brief moments of the rough handling, then the tender holding unleashed whatever emotions were bottled up inside her.

She wanted him, needed to feel his naked body on top of her body, wanted to feel helpless in his embrace, to feel his tongue on every ridge of her mouth, his lips on her proud nipples, and to feel his cock in her deeply flushed, suddenly wet pussy. She needed them to come together, to embrace him back into her body, possess him again, wash away the other men she'd pleasured last night, flush out every memory of them and their manliness. She wanted his hot semen blasting her vage filling her with his swimmers, reclaiming dominion over her body. She wanted, no, she craved his manliness there, thrusting, pushing, ramming, jamming, and flushing out all others.

They made long, lingering love; tongue kisses reaching for the deepest, innermost recesses, thrusting when his Big Willy could thrust no more, when the humping fell limp, and the writhing ceased, and when the gasping for breath eased, they simply dissolved into each other.

The phone rang . . . and rang, waking Kevin from his exhaustion. Finally the machine picked up the call.

"Girlfriend, call me," was all it said. Amy was sound asleep. After a short nap, Kevin quietly made his way out to his GLK, with his party clothes under his arm and drove home to his apartment.

Amy's phone rang again and the machine again did its job. It was Betty, better known as Grammy, "We're going to supper at the church at 6:30, and we'll drop the kids off on our way over there, ok? Love you, bye."

Sometime after noon, Amy stirred, got up, showered and put on fresh, clean clothes with no makeup. She was back in her "mom's role," and called Heather back.

"What's swinging Heath?" Using her code name for girl talk, Aim of course was Amy's. "You must be wiped from last night."

"No, not really last night, I guess we were too tired, but this morning . . . powerful and lovely loving, you?"

"Aim, last night, after we got home, it was like . . . I don't know . . . like we connected better than usual. I realized how much I do love Jeff and just being with those others made me feel it so much more. Sex is just sex, but after sex there is the love that floods in like high-tide creeping up on the shore, wave after wave, some gentle swells, some waves breaking, but all reaching higher and higher."

"Heath . . . spoken like a true poet, you should write this stuff down."

"I know."

"Listen, my kids will be home late this afternoon, but before then do you think we could get together at Michelle's house, maybe have a swim and bring her up to speed about all she missed yesterday . . . I want her there with us next time, don't you?"

"Sure, I don't see why not, see if you can get her on the phone-three way."

"Ok, . . . hold on, It's ringing . . . "Hello."

"Hi Dan, it's Heather, is Michelle there?"

"Sure, just a sec . . . honey it's Heather, for you."

"Hi Heath, how was your night out . . . or . . . whatever?"

"Fab, fab, fabulous . . . can't wait to tell you all about it . . . listen Mich, I've got Amy on the line too."

"Hi Mich."

"Hi yourself. What's up . . . you guys ganging up on me?"

"No, no of course not. Amy and I just have a lot to talk about, you know . . . about the party last night, and we thought why not share it with you in your pool this afternoon, if you're interested and not busy, of course."

"Sure, come on over. Dan's going down to his boat, meeting your Jeff there, something about it needing two of them to do something, I don't know . . . Dan's getting ready to go now. Come on over anytime, I'm dying to hear your story, or stories . . . whatever."

"Ok . . . Ok with you Aim?"

"Sure, see you there."

A few minutes later Jeff left for the marina to help Dan change the two big batteries in his boat. They were heavy, awkward and of course located down low in the bilge of the boat, hard to get at and harder still to lift out. After getting them out they needed to somehow put the new ones back in without dropping them or damaging something. It took a while with lots of grunts and cussing, damming the boat builders who made this process so difficult. Eventually it got done and after cleaning up the boat and themselves, they walked over to the marina's Dockside Grille for a well-deserved sandwich and beer.

"Ok, buddy, better start from the beginning and tell me all about this swinging stuff, I'm buying," Dan said,

"And don't leave anything out."

With a couple of Rueben's with fries, washed down with a pair of 16 oz. draft Docksider IPA's, Jeff spilled out their story of the past couple of weeks, pretty much covering all the activities; the orientation, the various women at the party, the group room (leaving out the part about Mark and Kevin) and spent a long time reliving for Jeff (and himself), his encounter with spectacular Susan. Peering from behind his bar, the barista probably thought they were gay, sitting so close together across the table and in deep conversation, ignoring everybody else in the place.

"But she was not slutty in any way," Jeff recalled beaming. "She was, so very much, the opposite. I felt as if I was in the hands of an expert mistress, a real sex-pert not that I've ever had one you know . . . but one who knew just what to do for me and to me, with none of the baggage that wives sometimes carry to bed. It was a great feeling, and I was so very sorry when we left that room. Who ever set it up knew what they were doing, it was small and simply furnished, but I remember the lighting bathed everything in a soft blue glow. It was the perfect make-out place without being frilly—you know stuff sitting around everywhere."

He went on, "I truly didn't want it to end, it was not like making love to Heather, I love her dearly and love getting it on with her, but with Susan, it seemed to be all about my making her happy and for her it was all about me. It was wild . . . he trailed off. I sure hope we can do it again," shaking his head slowly with a faraway look in his eyes.

"Did you feel guilty in any way, I mean, were you thinking about Heather all the time or did you feel like you were cheating on her . . . were you cheating on her?"

"No, no, not at all." Honestly, the only time I thought about Heather in there with Susan, was to want her there with us. I had a really strong desire to have them both by my side, you know, that warm loving feeling after a good fuck, you know . . . sure you want to sleep, but you also feel really attached to . . . to the person next to you, the person you love."

Finally, there was little more to say, but some of it Dan wanted to hear twice. He got up, paid their bill and each headed home filled with their own thoughts, Jeff re-remembering what he had just told Dan, and Dan thinking over what he had just heard. Could it be as simple and easy as Jeff had said . . . with the questions compounding on themselves. *Free to fuck anybody? Unreal!*

Dan parked his truck facing out in his driveway, making it easier leaving for work tomorrow. He should put it in the garage but his half of their two car garage was filled with Michelle's boxes of coats and clothes she was collecting for her "Native American kids" coming school year. It didn't matter if his truck sat outside; this truck had been his father's truck, an old classic Chevy step-side, short bed. Another day (or month) outside wouldn't do it any more weather damage than it already had. He'd bought the truck at the family farm estate auction in Illinois after his father died. Buying it from the executor eased whatever pain or jealously his brothers and sister might have for his having their daddy's old truck. He wanted to keep it in the family and restore it but had not yet found the time to begin.

He was not thinking of the truck as he walked through the house. His mind filled with vivid images of what awaited if he and Michelle could get invited to one of those swinging parties. He saw her on the covered patio behind their house and stopped long enough in the kitchen to open a long neck from the fridge. Then going out he sat with her, "So, what did you do all afternoon while I was working on that damn hot boat?" Her blouse was loose and he could tell she was not wearing a bra (men notice these things). It appeared she had sunburn that hadn't been there this morning.

7

THREE OF A KIND

EARLIER THAT SUNDAY, by the time Amy arrived at Michelle's house, Dan had already left to the marina taking his truck and leaving his usual oil stained spot on the driveway. She parked there. The side yard gate was standing open leading to the pool cage. Landscaping effectively blocked the pool and the neighbor's view of Michelle, already stretched out on their big double chase, with the paper's Sunday magazine in her hands, wearing, Amy noted with some pleasure, her thong bikini. A pitcher of iced tea and glasses sat on a tray beside her. The perfect picture of a Southern Belle with her beautiful full body and just a hint of duskiness blending and smoothing her tan.

Michelle waved Amy in, got up, gave her a quick hug then poured her a glass of Southern sweet tea. Amy shucked her T-shirt and the shorts she wore to drive here, covering her Brazilian bikini, the one she previously bought to match Michelle's. She had only worn it here once and once on their boat. The thong covered very little and the top was hardly there, just enough to make an intriguing tan line on her firm little tatas. Amy reached to get the tea, and as she leaned over Michelle, smiled and gave her a quick peck on her lips, "Love you!"

"Easy girl, you are too hot today. Better get some of this ice tea in you and cool off!" Michelle was a bit flustered by the kiss, "Is this left over from your party last night?"

"No, I just felt like it. Okay?"

"Of course, It's ok, I love you too."

"The party was . . . great. How can I describe something so totally different, free and wonderful, besides that it was so cool. Imagine, going to a place where you can flirt with anyone and have sex with anyone there and nobody cares, nobody is jealous?"

"But it was just a party, no?" Michelle had a bit of Latin blood in her veins and every once in awhile her expressions awoke some of that heritage.

"It was just a party, yes . . . but I'd be willing to bet money it was one unlike any you have ever been to."

Amy went on, "For sure, I've never been to one like it. You know how sometimes you are at a gathering and see some very interesting man . . . or woman . . . someone there that you'd like to get closer to, like a hug or a kiss or two, maybe a quiet romantic encounter, with no regrets or no after effects . . . well this place is like that. There you have permission to have your romantic encounter with anyone you like, if they like you of course, and no baggage afterward; no guilt, no recriminations, no consequences. It was like being on a different planet, an alternate world perhaps. And there were some really, really interesting people there, both men and women."

"Like who, anyone we know?"

"Like us mostly. No one I knew except for Heather and Jeff and Julie, you know our stylist. There were a dozen or more couples, one or two younger than us, maybe in their late twenties or early thirties and several our age and older, but not too old, maybe late fifties at the most. There wasn't anyone there I couldn't be friends with, at least I don't think so. There were no singles, everybody married or long term couples . . . well, except for one woman who had been in the club from the beginning with her husband, and he died young unexpectedly. The members asked her to continue coming, she was like family, and she helped out with the food and drinks, Rose is her name, a nice lady."

"So what did you do, did you kiss anyone besides Kevin?"

"Michelle, I didn't kiss Kevin at all last night."

"You what! Did you kiss anybody . . . what did you do then . . . y-you don't mean the big nasty?"

"Yes I did, I had a very exciting, very loving encounter with a man named Chad, and then another with Jim and his wife in the pool."

"And Kevin let you . . . two men?"

"Mich, Kevin was not involved, he was making love to that other lady, Rose, the one I just mentioned, and then we went to the group room and he and another guy got it on there, just from watching the action going on in the room."

The screen door squeaked opened. "Hey, what's happening you two, you're huddling and clucking like a pair of old hens," Heather said coming through.

"Amy's got me hotter than a . . . I don't know what . . . telling me about your party. Is it really true what she's saying?"

"Well, I don't know what she's told you, but it's all true, maybe even more so. Michelle, there is a whole new world of love, sex and special friends around us that we had no idea existed," she said putting her stuff down on a chase lounge.

"It was like going to a farmers fruit stand where every man and woman is a luscious, ripe, juicy morsel, shined and polished, just waiting to be sampled."

"Really? That's hot!" Michelle continued breathlessly, "Of course I've heard of swing clubs, but aren't they just sleazy pick-up places for horny guys and prostitutes?"

"Maybe some are, but the Palms isn't. That's what they call it, the club, the group . . . the Palms. It's a totally different thing, and it's not far from here, just a regular house, much like yours only larger maybe, with a pool and hot tub. Angelea and Robert hold their parties there, he's in his fifties I'd say, but good looking, well toned and his wife, Angelea, is beautiful, middle forties I think, wouldn't you say Amy?"

"They are a good looking couple, yes absolutely. I'd like to make love to him sometime."

"Maybe you will, Amy, maybe you will," Heather smiled knowingly as she gave Amy a hug lasting a split second longer than necessary, sisters now.

"Huh, am I missing something here?" Michelle was all attention again . . . then,

"I'm sorry, I forgot my manners, tea, Heather?" Michelle got up and poured a glass for Heather and topped up Amy's ice tea as well.

Heather too, had a bikini under her t-shirt top and peeling the shirt off revealed a full body needing nothing except perhaps someone to love and caress it often.

"Mmmm—you're looking good Heather," as Michelle gave her a hug that lasted a second or two longer than usual, then, sensing it was time to change the chit-chat to some real women's talk, Michelle sat the ice tea pitcher down.

"Ok, now you two have to tell me everything. I've been on the edge of crazy since our boat ride and you dumped your bombshell on me. But first let's all get naked and grab some rays, Dan won't be back for hours."

She reached behind her back and untied her bra string ties then added it to the tee shirt on the foot of her chaise.

"There, I feel so much better free of clothes," Michelle stretched and stepping to a patio table, "There's sunscreen and lotion here, better put some on, we'll all need some today." Michelle's body reflected her pool time with bikini lines outlining her petite boobs and heart shaped tush.

With only a moment's hesitation, Amy and Heather pared off their bikini tops as well and began slathering sunscreen and lotion on their arms and legs. When that was done, they covered each other's back and body parts that were hard to reach or nice to touch, nay-nays and nipples especially. Conversation slowed and then stopped to be replaced by o-h-h-o's and ah-h-a's. The girls enjoying the touching as much as being touched, lovingly as any three good friends could, if they only would. After a bit of standing around spreading sunscreen, Michelle spread towels on the big double chase, then perched on the edge and continued the touching, rubbing and massaging. This went on long past the time required to apply sunscreen and tension built until Amy turned and leaning over, kissed Heather lightly on her cheek who surprised, didn't react right away but after a moment turned and kissed her back, but full on the lips, holding it and teasing with her darting tongue in and out, drinking Amy in. Michelle was watching and although she had kissed and been kissed by each of the others, somehow this was different. They were onto something . . . and she wanted in, she was a friend too.

Moving closer, Michelle lightly drew her finger tips across Amy's cheek who, surprised, turned to face her and then let her own hand drift to Michelle, caressing neck and shoulders, teasing, testing, then leaning over her she kissed the slender column of her throat . . . Amy's eyes flushing, a wellspring of want, pleading for a kiss which came quickly from Michelle's lusting lips, that opened to Amy, holding nothing back. Arms joined their heated flesh as the kiss fused and held. When they kiss your neck you instantly feel it between your legs.

Heather, startled by her own primitive, feminine need, rained kisses across Michelle's silky shoulder and molded intimately against her, touching and wanting to become a part of the union before her. With her breasts tight against Michelle, the three began slowly moving which was picked up, passed along, and then started again. The three girls were like one body with multiple arms and legs, twisting, turning, pleasuring and loving, eyes closed against the hot sun, going on until Michelle had to gasp and began to moan . . . someone was touching her muffin, gently massaging with a pair of fingers that now moved under her bikini, other fingers explored her vadge, bringing a rush of anticipation before finding her clit. She had never had another woman's touch there, much less two. The pleasure sensations came in ripples, flushes, building into a burgeoning frenzy of drugging waves, giving her one convulsing orgasm after another that had her clutching her partners and her pussy until . . . spent, she collapsed full out on the chase.

No one spoke, they couldn't, too exhausted, and too shocked, too . . . much! Eventually, Michelle disentangled herself from the arms and legs on the chase and walked over to the outdoor shower, rinsed herself off then sat on the pool edge for a moment before letting herself slip in the cool water . . . ah-h, relief! Heather and Amy soon followed, also slipping in the pool beside her. Then, with their arms loosely around each other, the three friends bobbed in the water like ducklings in a pond. They could not stop grinning.

Finally Michelle got out; dried off, wrapped herself in the towel then sat on the edge of the pool feet in the water.

"It's a good thing Jeff and Dan aren't back from the boat, especially not while we were . . . busy. I'm not sure Dan's ready for his wife getting it on with girls, Michelle said laughing, but I sure enjoyed it."

"He might surprise you," Amy piped up.

"At the Palms there was some girl on girl in the group room and it didn't seem to bother him, in fact I think it contributed to Kevin's jacking off with Mark."

"He what!"

Heather laughed, "That's another story for another time."

She remembered how easy it was to just let go and enjoy the one you were with, forgetting husbands, boundaries, and conventions and societies no-nos. The Palms parties were a lot more the way life should be lived; open, accepting, honest, giving and inclusive. It's odd to think of one's life in that way, but we all live within society's strict boundaries. Being open and without boundaries, offers so much more of life.

"So, tell me about the . . . palms," Michelle said,

"I want to know everything."

♥

End of Book One

Book Two of this series is available where you got this one.

I hope you enjoy the continuing saga of my Sophisticated Swingers.

Book Three is in production.

Thanks for reading.

Follow our adventures from my Blog

www.sophisticatedswingers.org

Chao everybody,

Michelle